DarkIsle:
Resurrection

D1149527

DarkIsle: Resurrection

D. A. Nelson

www.stridentpublishing.co.uk

Published by
Strident Publishing Ltd
22 Strathwhillan Drive
The Orchard, Hairmyres
East Kilbride G75 8GT

Tel: +44 (0)1355 220588
info@stridentpublishing.co.uk
www.stridentpublishing.co.uk

A catalogue record for this book is
available from the British Library.

ISBN 978-1-905537-18-1

The publisher acknowledges subsidy from the Scottish
Arts Council towards the publication of this volume.

Typeset in Lucida Bright
Designed by Sallie Moffat

D. A. Nelson

was born in Glasgow and grew up in Neilston.

On leaving school she became a trainee reporter, working for various newspapers in Central Scotland, before moving into PR. She started writing at an early age, and still has a pile of books she wrote as a child. She loves books and her favourite pastime is sitting in a bookstore, cup of tea and muffin to hand, reading a fantastic new novel.

The *DarkIsle* trilogy was inspired by a huge stone dragon that overlooks Irvine Beach on Scotland's west coast. The sculpture was created by Roy Fitzsimmons.

D. A. Nelson lives in Cardross, Scotland. She is currently working on the third *DarkIsle* novel.

In memory of my friends,
Katrina Grant and Anna Lauw,
two wonderful women who
will never be forgotten.

With thanks to

Keith, Graham and Alison at Strident for all
their support over the past few years; to all the
DarkIsle fans (young and old) I've met during my
travels; to Ian for making me sit at my computer
when I'd rather watch tv.

chapter one

350 years ago

Breathless and desperate, the boy staggered across the beach. The hard sand was covered in broken shells that jabbed his feet like tiny knives. He ignored the pain and took a deep breath of the fresh sea air. Overhead, gulls screeched: *fool, fool, fool!* He closed his ears to their goading and tried to clear his head.

His knuckles began to throb again. The numbness that had spread after the punch had subsided and he clasped his fist to dull the ache. He was cold and sore and hungry. But he was free, and his father would never hurt him again. The boy smiled as he remembered the blow he had landed on his old man's stupid face. His father had been on at him again, calling him a fool and pushing him around to go out and bring money in to feed his thirst.

'You're a lazy good-for-nothing boy!'

The words still echoed around James's head and he shut his eyes, squeezing with all his might to rid them from his mind, but he could not purge himself of the memory of the wicked look in his father's eyes, as the man once more raised his fist. Even the thought of it made him catch his breath and his eyes flew open in terror.

He looked around, his heart beating ten to the dozen, scared he was being followed. The beach was empty save for a few sea birds digging for razor clams. The only sounds were the calming whoosh of the waves as they smoothed the sand.

The punch had been totally out of character for James. Normally, he would have taken the beating, but something inside him had snapped. He had decided he would never suffer at his father's hands again. So, he had knocked him down and run out of their tiny farmhouse forever. To go where, he didn't know.

Now he found himself on a beach, kicking up stones and wondering what to do next. He couldn't go home, no matter how hard his mother pleaded, so the only alternative was to go south to seek his fortune.

Roawwwl.

His stomach grumbled, reminding him he had not eaten yet. Not that hunger was unusual. His father drank the few pennies he and his brothers and sisters made from working the land, so there was never enough food. However, today was the start of his new life and he wasn't about to start it hungry. He searched for a good sharp stone to prize the limpets off the jagged rocks. A few looked promising, but as he lifted them he knew they would shatter. On the other side of the beach he spied the perfect specimen. It was a large flattish stone lying at the shallow end of one of the larger rock pools. He bent down, scooped it out of the icy water and weighed it in his hand. It was solid. Perfect. He smiled. The prospect of eating those limpets sent his brain into a frenzy of longing.

He was about to walk away from the rock pool to collect some driftwood for a fire when something else under the water, something large and smooth and very white, caught his eye. What was it? It glowed enticingly, almost as if calling to him. Without thinking, he knelt by the edge of the pool and plunged his arm in. There was something strange about this particular stone. It was *warm*, and as his fingers wrapped around it, the stone began to glimmer as though a shaft of light had struck it. It made a buzzing sound that intensified as it was pulled from the water. James stared at it in astonishment. It was a smooth lozenge-shaped stone, a little bigger than a rugby ball and unlike anything he had seen before. The buzzing grew even louder and the stone's light even brighter, until suddenly there was a flash and the boy was thrown backwards onto the sand. He momentarily blacked out.

'Are you all right, lad?' a stranger's voice said from somewhere far away.

The boy dragged himself back to consciousness. His eyes fluttered open and he looked at the kindly face peering down at him. He nodded dumbly.

'You've found it!' said the man staring in wonder at the stone in James's hands. 'There were legends of it falling from the sky. Such a bright light, our ancestors said. And they searched the sea for it. The tides must have washed it ashore. What's your name?' The man's green eyes sparkled as he helped the boy to sit up.

'James, sir,' the boy replied weakly. 'James Montgomery.'

'Colm Breck,' replied the man, holding out a hand of friendship. As James went to take it, the man unexpectedly fell to his knees. 'Hail young James Montgomery: Finder of the Eye of Lornish!'

Marnoch Mor. Now.

The dodo frowned and waggled his tail feathers as he read and then re-read the online article. A ritualistic dagger in a human museum had, according to the only witness—a white-faced curator—simply vanished before his eyes. *Nothing vanishes in the human world*, the dodo thought, *without something being affected here*, and he clicked the video link to pick up more clues from the interview.

The curator was a thin man with wispy yellow hair and a squirming nervousness that made Bertie flinch with embarrassment for him. Wringing the bottom of his jacket with his hands, the man related his extraordinary tale. He had been on his usual late-night rounds checking the exhibits when he had stopped in the armoury section. In the dim light the gleaming dagger, housed in an unbreakable glass case, had caught his attention.

'I went over to look at it, to check it was all right and then...well...I watched it vanish like a wisp of smoke,' he told the interviewer, his eyes darting about apprehensively. 'One minute it was there, the next it wasn't. Pop, it was gone. I've never seen anything like it before in my life,' he continued. 'It was almost as if it was *magic*.'

Bertie's little dodo eyes narrowed. *Magic? In the human world?* He hoped not. The video clip showed the empty glass case as a grim-faced blond reporter closed the story.

'Police are baffled by the incident and con-firm that the museum's security systems show no-one broke into the building,' she said. 'One thing's for sure, this will go down as one of the most puzzling disappearances of this century...'

The dodo stared at the screen for a few sec-onds before closing the link. This was all wrong. '*It was almost as if it was magic.*' The curator's final words jigged about in his head and he frowned. If magic had been used, why would someone from his world need a ritualistic dagger from a human museum? There were many excel-lent shops in Marnoch Mor where you could get anything you wanted, including magical daggers. It didn't make sense.

He slid from his chair and grabbed a bundle of

news stories he had printed off earlier. He shuffled over to a large red sofa wedged up against the far wall and took from its broad back a yellow ring-binder marked: '*Weird happenings of the human world*'. He opened it and placed the cuttings inside: '*Cursed Egyptian Charm Disappears*' read one; '*No Clues to Whereabouts of Priceless Jade Cup*' read another; '*Reward for Return of Ancient Spell Book*' said the third. They had all gone missing in the last two days and Bertie was beginning to feel uneasy about what that might mean.

He closed his folder with a snap and returned it to the sofa. He yawned. This would have to wait until the morning; it was too late to do anything about it tonight. Maybe if he slept on it, a pattern behind the disappearances might come to him. With that thought, he left his study and made his way down the hallway.

Bertie's little round bedroom was opposite the study. Without switching the light he removed his Cosy-Claws slippers, pulled on his tartan nightshirt and drew back the duvet. He hopped into bed and cuddled down. Within seconds, he was asleep and snoring.

***

Bang, bang, bang!

Bertie forced open his eyes and grimaced. *What now?* he thought, sitting up and ruffling his feathers.

Bang, bang, bang.

A muffled voice seemed to be calling his name. The dodo glanced at his bedside clock: it was seven o'clock in the morning. Who would be calling at this time?

With a dark cloud of irritation hanging over him, the bird got out of bed and stomped out into the hallway.

'Lights!' he squawked and the hallway was immediately lit by the soft glow of a hundred little Moonstones sunk into the ceiling. Muttering angrily to himself about rude people waking him up too early, he made his way to the front door.

Bertie lived in a burrow under a grand old oak tree. Gnarly as a witch's hands, the tree stood in the middle of The Oval, Marnoch Mor's park. The dodo wasn't the only resident of this large green space; fairies, elves, and wood nymphs had houses in the trees, or under them, and their lives were taken up with making The Oval as beautiful as possible.

His burrow went far below ground, stretching between the tree roots, and over the years he had dug out new rooms when he felt he needed them. So far, the burrow had a bedroom, a study, a large kitchen, a living room and a guest room (although Bertie was always too busy to entertain). A long tunnel led from the bedroom up to a round front door cut into the base of the tree. The door was grass-green, with a brass plate which announced his full name: *Albert Alonzo*

Fluke, Trainee Wizard.

It also had a brass door knocker shaped like a pineapple which someone was currently banging very hard while shouting his name through the letterbox.

'All right, all right, I'm coming!' he yelled.

'Bertie! Hurry up. I must speak to you!'

Ever cautious, the dodo squinted through the letterbox. All he could see were black shiny buttons and a fuzzy red coat.

'Who is it?' he called, his voice wavering. 'Stand back and show yourself!'

The person bent down quickly and a pair of blue eyes stared back at him.

The bird shrieked with fright and fell backwards to the floor, clasping his downy chest with a wing and breathing rapidly.

'It's me—Morag,' she said. 'Are you all right?'

'I'm...fine...fine...' the bird spluttered. He sat up and dusted down his trembling feathers. 'You just gave me a bit of a turn, that's all.'

'Sorry...I didn't mean to...look, will you let me in! There's something I need to speak to you about!'

Breathing deeply to calm his rapidly beating heart, and with one wing fanning his hot beak, he shakily stood up and unlocked the door.

'Come in,' he said as the cold November air blasted him.

Morag didn't need a second invitation and scuttled into the warmth. Ever cautious, Bertie took a quick look outside to check that she hadn't been followed. Despite it being morning, it was dark and grey. There was a sharpness in the air that Bertie knew heralded the winter's first snow.

'I didn't know who else to talk to,' a rosy-cheeked Morag said as she took off her red duffle coat and white bobble hat and hung them on the coat-stand. 'Shona would only panic.'

'Oh no. Has it happened again?' Bertie asked.

The girl nodded. She patted her pocket. 'I've written everything down,' she said.

They sat at Bertie's big wooden table and, as the dodo made tea, Morag pulled out a battered leather-bound book. It was the only reminder she had of her parents, who had left it with her before they disappeared when she was a baby. She fished out a piece of paper from between the pages and handed it to him.

Bertie took it and read it, his eyes widening at every sentence.

'Another dream about the drowned maid from Murst,' he said when he'd finished. He folded it over and handed it back to Morag. 'How many is that now?'

'Five,' replied Morag with a stifled sob, 'but this was the worst. She says my life is in danger and I am going to be joining her soon.'

'But why should you take them seriously? They're only nightmares, just like the ones you had after you killed Devlish.'

'I didn't kill him, the Eye of Lornish did it,' she

said firmly. 'Oh Bertie, they are so real. I wake up shaking after every one.'

'And it's definitely *her*?'

'Yes, she told me how she died. She said Mephista had chained her up and dropped her into the sea near the jetty.'

'But why is she coming to you? You didn't know her,' said the dodo, pouring her a cup of tea. Morag took it gratefully.

'It must have something to do with the Eye of Lornish,' she replied. 'The night Devlish was killed on the jetty something strange happened to me. I can't quite explain it, but since then I've been dreaming about dead people. I talk to them in my dreams. I'm scared, Bertie. What am I going to do?'

'I've never come across anything like this before,' he replied. 'And it cannot be ignored. The time has come to tell Shona, whatever your misgivings. She is your guardian after all. Hopefully she'll know what to do...'

chapter two

Shona was in her kitchen when Morag and Bertie arrived. She was polishing the bright buckle of her Special Chief Constable's helmet. The Marnoch Mor Volunteer Police Force had been set up by Montgomery after the theft of the Eye of Lornish. The evil warlock Devlish had spirited it away to his lair on the DarkIsle of Murst. From there, he had planned to use its magic to enslave Marnoch Mor and attack the human world. Without its protection Marnoch Mor had been thrown into chaos and had started to crumble. Montgomery was certain that if it hadn't been for Morag and her friends the stone would never have been restored to its rightful place at the top of Marnoch Mor's tallest tower. He had established the Police Force to ensure it would never happen again, giving his trusted friend Shona the dragon the top job. Although at this stage the Volunteers were still a straggly group of well-meaning townspeople led by a grumpy dragon, it was just as well he had done this, for the evil powers on the DarkIsle continued to threaten them. Both Montgomery and Shona were convinced of that. And so they kept a watchful eye on the town, each in their own way.

'Hello Bertie,' Shona said as the dodo entered the room. She gave the brass buckle one final rub before quickly plonking the hat on her head. 'Sorry, I can't stay and chat. Got my first job as a detective. Something has disappeared from the Museum of Weird Things and Magic.'

'But…' started Morag. 'We need to speak to you. It's important!'

'Can't it wait 'til later?' the dragon asked, opening the back door.

'No, we need to speak to you now!' Morag insisted.

'Her life might be in danger,' the dodo added.

Shona narrowed her large yellow eyes. Muriel Burntwood, the curator of the Museum of Weird Things and Magic, had told Shona she was needed urgently as something extremely dangerous had been stolen. But now her best friend was looking frightened for her life. What should she do and who should she help first? She chewed her lip and let a spiral of smoke escape from her nostril in frustration.

'Come with me and you can tell me about it on the way,' she said as she led them into the garden.

The Museum was not far from Morag and Shona's cottage and unfortunately it was quicker to walk than to order the Super Glider service, where a witch would pick you up at your front door on a hover bike and drop you off at your destination. Shona led the friends towards the gate, past a castle-shaped birdhouse on top of a tall pole. Here Morag stopped, and before Shona had time to complain the girl yanked a rope that was hanging down. A bell tinkled in the silence of the wintery garden.

From inside the birdhouse came sounds of scuffling and scratching. Then a window shutter opened and a pink nose and pair of whiskers twitched in the cold air.

'Who is it? Why did you wake me? Is it spring yet?' a yawning rat was heard to say.

'No, we can't wait until spring,' called Morag. 'Get dressed and come down quickly!'

Aldiss poked his hairy face out and blinked. When he saw how troubled his friends looked he disappeared back inside, calling, 'I'll be there in just a moment.'

***

Seconds later he bounded out, dressed for the weather: a neon-pink bobble hat on his head (with two holes for his ears to stick through) and a matching scarf casually slung around his neck. On his legs, he wore fuchsia-coloured legwarmers. 'Ready!' Aldiss squeaked as he scampered down to the ground. 'Let's go.'

Bertie was appalled. 'If this wasn't an emergency I'd insist you go back up there and change...'

As they walked, Morag told Shona and Aldiss how she'd dreamed about the ghostly maid, and how her terrible warnings had frightened her. The dragon listened quietly, taking in all the details.

'Talking to spooks in your dreams?' wondered Aldiss, whiskers twitching. 'Is that even possible?'

Shona frowned. 'Back on Murst in the old days they said it was possible, but such things were outlawed by the time I was a dragonlet. I can't believe you didn't tell me before,' she scolded. 'We could have done something about it.'

Morag looked crestfallen. Sighing, the dragon took pity on her. 'Montgomery must be told,' Shona said firmly. 'He'll know how best to keep you safe while I investigate.'

'And who's the suspect?' cried Aldiss excitedly.

'That's the trouble,' Shona said. 'If someone is sending you bad dreams they're bending the laws and using powerful old magic to do it.'

'But who would do such a thing?' asked Morag.

Shona placed a huge claw around her small shoulders and gave the worried girl a hug. 'Don't worry about it Morag, we'll get to the bottom of this. In the meantime, I want you to stick closely to me. I'll protect you. No-one's going to try anything while I'm here.'

Morag smiled at her and felt a bit better.

They turned the corner and set off down Merlin's Walk, Marnoch Mor's main street. The scent of freshly made Snook Bread wafted towards them from Patty the Hag's Patisserie. Patty sold a wide range of strange but tasty pastries, including Morag's favourite: Exploding Donuts, which crackled in your mouth and turned into stars.

Morag could not help noticing how quiet the town had become. Yes, there was a bitter wind whistling between the buildings, but that normally didn't put people off. The streets were usually heaving, yet that morning only a handful of townsfolk were about. Even outside Erbium Smyte's Department Store, which sold '*Everything You Never Knew You Wanted*', they saw hardly a soul. A lone dodo carrying an empty wicker basket scuttled by; a unicorn stared at top hats in the milliner's window and a tiny flower elf, smaller even than Aldiss, cried out indignantly when Morag nearly stood on him as he waited for a Super Glider. But that was it.

Mrs Milda's Old Fashioned Coffee Shoppe ('*Concessions for those over 200*'), usually packed, was deserted when they looked in its bay window. *Strange*, thought Morag, *where is everyone? It's Thursday and the streets are always busier than this.* She dismissed her worries for the moment as they reached the Museum of Weird Things and Magic, the town's oldest building.

Three hundred and fifty years ago it had been Colm Breck's cottage, where he had hidden magical folk fleeing the human world. Up until then they had lived peacefully with humans. Then one of their own, a warlock named Devlish the First, had persuaded men that magic folk and strange beasts should serve humans. Kelpies, witches and elves were rounded up and unicorns and satyrs were hunted. Those who escaped headed north as word spread that there was only one place left to hide: a tiny cottage in a clearing behind the mountains.

As more came to Colm Breck, he built a couple of shacks near his own, and then a few more appeared, until a little village had grown up around him. Knowing that Devlish and his tribe would seek them out, Colm Breck used the Eye of Lornish to create a shield around the settlement to make it invisible.

Many years passed and Marnoch Mor grew. Beautiful larger houses, made from sandstone and slate, were built; a palace was created for Marnoch Mor's first ruler Adela Augusta, its towers and spires stretching higher than any in the human world; and the streets, paved and clean, ran straight. By then, Colm Breck's old house was falling down; its roof was rotting and its door was hanging off its hinges. A small army of magical people took it upon themselves to do something about it. Together, they raised their wands and prepared to bring it down.

But Queen Adela had intervened, crying, 'Stop! Leave the building as a monument to the past. Let us turn it into a museum so that none of us may forget what has happened and where we came from.'

A murmur had risen from the crowd: 'That

wasn't such a bad idea,' said some; 'Saves us clearing it away,' said others; 'We could use a museum,' said a few more.

And so the Museum of Weird Things and Magic came to be housed in the one of the smallest and most rickety buildings Morag had ever seen. Its single storey appeared to have one-room, and the whole place was made of rotting planks of wood...or so it seemed to Morag as she followed Shona up the groaning stairs to the front door. The smell of mould and damp was overwhelming.

The dragon raised a claw and gently tapped.

'Who's there?' came a woman's voice, as creaky as the building.

'Shona of the Volunteer Police Force!' the dragon announced.

With an ear-piercing squeal from the hinges, the door opened to reveal a short tubby woman dressed in grey robes. Her wispy hair was streaked with white and held in an untidy knot on top of her head by two knitting needles. A pair of spectacles hung around her neck on a gold chain, and a ginger cat mewed loudly at her feet. She held a wooden wand in one hand.

'Elma MacPhail, Assistant Curator,' she said, introducing herself. 'Come and wait inside while I fetch Muriel.'

Morag stepped through the doorway and looked around, astonished. 'It was tiny on the outside...' she gasped. She could hardly believe her eyes:

they were standing in a vast, domed hallway at least twice as high as the roof they had seen from the street. A polished floor stretched before them to marble pillars and a sweeping staircase that Elma was busy hollering up: *'Murrrieeeelll!!!'*

On the walls were huge paintings of famous Marnoch Morians, including the green-eyed hero Colm Breck and—Morag was interested to see— Montgomery, wearing what she supposed was fancy dress, for he had on breeches and an old-fashioned tail coat. A large chandelier hung from the high ceiling and light flooded in through tall arched windows.

'Murrrrieeellll!!!' screeched Elma again. 'Visi-torrrrsssss!' She turned to the others and smiled sweetly. 'She'll be here in a minute.'

No sooner had the words left her lips than a puff of pink smoke drifted down the staircase and formed a tall column on the last step. As they watched, the smoke condensed, until it solidified into a smiling woman in a long cerise gown. She looked older than Elma but obviously spent a lot of time taking care of herself, for her long blond hair had been pinned into an immaculate helmet shape on her head. Pearls hung from her neck and precious stones adorned her many rings.

'Muriel Burntwood,' she smiled, shaking Morag's hand. 'Pleased to meet you, Shona.'

'Oh, I'm not...' began the flustered girl.

'*I'm* Shona!' snapped the dragon, elbowing her way to the front.

Muriel looked down her long nose at the dragon, her face pursed into a tight knot. 'Oh, but you're a...dragon,' she sneered.

'Is that a problem?' Shona growled.

'It's just that I didn't expect the head of the Police Force to be a...well...to be a...' There was a pause as everyone waited to hear what she would say next. 'A *reptile*,' she hissed.

Morag, Bertie and Aldiss gasped as Shona's nostrils began to smoke. But Muriel didn't seem to notice. 'But I suppose you can't help that,' she continued, 'so you'll have to do.' She turned on her high heels and began to walk upstairs. 'Follow me.'

Click, click, click. Her shoes tapped off the marble. She glanced behind her and saw no-one was following.

'Come on! Chop chop!' she called, clapping her hands. 'You've wasted enough time as it is!'

'Just ignore her, Shona,' Morag said quietly as the dragon's green scaly face turned red with rage. 'She's just a silly woman who needs you more than you need her.'

'One more 'chop' from her and she'll be barbequed,' rasped the dragon.

Morag began to climb the stairs, with Bertie behind and Aldiss scampering on ahead. She motioned for the dragon to follow and, face like thunder, she did.

Muriel took them up, past level after level. It seemed as if the staircase would never end.

Morag had never been in a building as tall as this before and longed to explore all the other floors.

At last, they came to a stop on a red carpeted landing. They had climbed thirteen flights and everyone, except Aldiss (who was doing star jumps), was puffed out. The Curator, however, was still as fresh as a Marnoch Mor daisy.

'This way,' she said, tottering towards two large white doors. 'Do be careful,' she added looking pointedly at Aldiss. 'And don't touch anything!' The rat looked shamefaced and removed his paw from a large vase standing next to him.

Muriel pushed open the doors and the visitors were immediately bathed in a pure, white light. It took some moments before they got used to the brightness, but when they did, Morag gasped. Stunned into silence, she walked into a space larger than a cathedral. Her mouth hung open— this place was *amazing*. Each room seemed bigger than the one before. The walls were crammed with rows of white shelves heaving under the weight of thousands of books of all shapes and sizes. The white light came from the Full Moonstones, glowing in constellations on the distant blue ceiling. Morag recognised Orion and The Plough, but not the others. She wondered if Marnoch Mor skies had their own stars.

Dotted between the bookshelves were exhibits in display cases. Morag looked into the nearest one and saw the gold bejewelled death mask of a long-forgotten Wizard Emperor. Beside it lay a pair of huge pink bloomers once worn by a giant-ess. On top of them a glass eye (used by the witch Baba Yaga, according to the card) stared as they went past. The rest of the case was taken up with a huge hen's claw, a golden goose egg, three swan feathers and a wooden pudding bowl and spoon.

On the walls of the library were the disembod-ied heads of long-extinct animals, which Bertie and Aldiss found distasteful and would not look at. Morag, however, was fascinated. The first was the head of an enormous hairy mammoth, its elephant-like face relaxed and its eyes closed as if it were sleeping. Morag thought she heard it snore and was about to walk on when the mam-moth head gave a resounding snort, mumbled something about getting dinner and went back to sleep. Next to it was the head of a fierce sa-bre-toothed tiger. Alert and growling quietly, it watched as the girl tip-toed around it. As she got a little too near, the tiger suddenly snapped its huge jaws, so close that Morag felt a draught an inch above her head.

'Watch Samson,' Muriel warned, a little too late. 'I'm afraid he's a bit of a biter! Now, where did we keep the tooth? Hmmmm....Ah, yes, follow me, it was over here!'

While the others followed, Morag found her-self drawn to the bookshelves. She had always loved reading and scanned the spines. '*One Thousand and One Ways to Remove Spell Stains,*' she read aloud.

'*The Swamp and Me: One Witch's Journey*'
'*I Was a Teenage Zombie*'
'*Taming Demons and Other Handy Tips for Life*'
'*My Dead Husband Came Back to Haunt Me and Now We're Renewing Our Wedding Vows.*'

Just then her eyes fell upon a set of small, red leather-bound books marked with a white card saying: '*Early Marnoch Mor poetry.*'

She held her breath: they looked remarkably familiar. They looked like...well, they looked like...she felt for her own book of poetry in her pocket. It was the only thing she had left of her parents; she treasured it like a good friend and never let it out of her sight. It was still there. *No, it couldn't be*, she thought, *I'm just being silly.* She dismissed the notion from her head and began to walk away, but the books seemed to be calling her back. Without quite knowing *what* she was searching for, Morag quickly looked over the book's spines. They were numbered 1 to 20 but there was a gap where number 13 should have been. Her heart skipped a beat. Hands trembling, she found herself reaching into her pocket. Slowly, she pulled out her own red leather-bound book and turned it around to examine the spine. Sure enough there was the faint outline of a 1 and a 3, which she had never noticed before. She opened it and stared at the first page. The unreadable ancient words now reformed in front of her eyes. *The Poetry of Marnoch Mor*, it said.

Morag's head was a blizzard of thoughts. How could her book be part of this set? That would mean her parents had once stood right here, and that they had taken the book to leave for her when she was a baby. Had they known she would find her way to Marnoch Mor? The enormity of this discovery overwhelmed her.

'Interested in poetry are we?' said a voice. Morag jumped. She turned to see the grey outline of the Assistant Curator at the door. She hastily stashed her book in her pocket.

'Oh yes, absolutely,' she answered. 'My parents liked it too. I used to read it at home.'

'That's the only set in existence you know,' Elma said, proudly running her fingers over the spines until she reached the gap. 'It's such a shame it's not complete.'

She gazed at Morag, as if she knew the girl was hiding something. Morag felt her face burn.

'Number Thirteen.' Elma continued, 'A terribly unlucky number...for some.'

Morag tried not to tremble. She shifted from foot to foot.

'Maybe someone who liked poetry forgot to bring it back? Maybe they couldn't remember where it came from?' she suggested.

'And remembering where something comes from is very important,' Elma said, leaning down to look right into Morag's eyes. 'Isn't it?'

'Well,' replied Morag. 'It helps...' Elma eyed her suspiciously and Morag winced under the intensity of her gaze. It was as if Elma was trying to peer into her soul.

Just as Elma opened her mouth to say something else, she was interrupted—much to Morag's relief—by Shona.

'What's the big secret?' Shona shouted. 'Stop whispering and come look at this.'

With a tight smile, Morag excused herself and hurried over to the far corner of the room where Shona, Muriel, Bertie and Aldiss were staring intently into an empty display case.

chapter three

'What do you make of this?' the dragon asked as Morag joined them.

'What is it?' asked Morag.

'Look!' said Aldiss pointing to a perfectly round hole cut in the glass lid. Underneath was a purple velvet cushion that had once held something very small and very 'not there-any-more'.

'It's a hole,' Morag shrugged. 'So what?'

'So what? So *what?*' shrieked Muriel throwing her hands in the air in frustration. 'Have you any idea what you're looking at?'

The girl shook her head. 'An empty cushion?' she ventured.

'On that cushion lay an item so old and so powerful it could raise the dead,' Muriel said with a shudder. 'The witch Mina McPhail's jagged tooth. It was rescued from her ashes after humans burned her at the stake in 1531. She made the mistake of eating three boys and half a girl.'

Morag's eyes widened.

'You must know the story of Hansel and Gretel?' Muriel continued. 'Where an old hag tries to fatten a poor little brother and sister so she can gobble them up?'

Morag nodded.

'That was based on Mina. She was always on the lookout for little lost children who had no-one to save them.'

Morag shifted nervously.

'If we don't get it back, someone may use the tooth for...well I dread to think what they'll use it for.'

Morag studied the hole again and frowned. If the tooth was so dangerous, what was it doing in a glass case in a museum? She was about to voice her concerns, when Shona did it for her.

'So,' said the dragon in her most professional Police Officer voice, 'how did the thief steal the tooth? Surely it was well guarded, or you were using security spells?'

'Well, yes,' Elma interrupted. 'I was on duty last night and we always make sure we have at least three security spells on the building so that no-one can get in. We've also got magical motion sensors on all the doors and staircases so that nothing can move from floor to floor, or from room to room. Or through walls. If something's detected, the perpetrator is immediately sprayed with a web that freezes them until the morning. Works a charm on moths too.'

'And did you see or hear anything unusual last night?' Shona went on. 'Was anything caught in the web?'

'No, nothing,' Elma replied, 'although the rats seemed worse than usual. Scuffling about all night they were. We'll need to get a Rat Catcher in to get rid of them.'

Aldiss bristled.

'Have you always had a problem with rats?' Morag asked.

'Why are you asking that?' Muriel snapped. 'What has that got to do with the theft of Mina's tooth?'

Morag was a little taken aback, but went on. 'Well, if you would answer my question, I'll tell you.'

'Please answer her,' Shona said.

Elma pursed her lips. 'No,' she replied. 'The problem only started about a week ago. But I've heard them every night.'

'Where are they at their worst?' the girl wanted to know.

'In the cellar,' replied the witch, 'where the drains go outside. And I've also heard them scuttling about in the air vents in…in…' The woman's face paled.

'*Where*?' Morag and Shona cried together.

'In this room…' she answered.

'Hmmm,' said Morag, 'interesting. And where is the air vent in this room?'

Elma did not speak, but pointed to a small grill fastened loosely on the wall, near the floor. Morag walked over and got down on her hands and knees to study it closely. She sniffed at the grill and the space around it. 'And have you actually *seen* these rats?' she asked sceptically.

Muriel, who did not like the way this was going,

frowned. She turned to the girl. 'Are you telling me you think rats stole the tooth?' she asked haughtily.

'No,' replied Morag, picking up something from the grill before scrambling to her feet. 'It's worse than that. I think a Klapp demon got in through the drains and into the air vents. It climbed up here, opened the grill, and broke into the case. Here's its fur snagged on the grill.' She held up a tuft of matted brown hair. 'And if you want further proof, have a sniff over here. You can still smell the rotten stench of Klapp demon.'

'That's preposterous!' Muriel sneered. 'Why didn't it get caught in the web?'

'Maybe it was using magic? Wouldn't be the first time,' replied Morag, 'It's something you'll have to look into.'

'Well done.' Shona smiled briefly and examined the fur in Morag's hands. 'I think you're right about it being a Klapp demon. You'll make a great Volunteer when you're older.'

Morag's heart swelled with pride. She was happy she had been of some help.

'Well...I...don't know about that...' spluttered Muriel. 'Our security spells are the best any magic has ever produced!'

'They are obviously not as foolproof as you think,' said Shona triumphantly.

'So now what?' asked Bertie, peering at the clump of fur.

Shona looked at Morag before answering. 'Let's

go to see Montgomery. There is only one reason why a Klapp demon would do this and that's because someone on Murst sent it,' she said. 'Besides, I have other business to discuss with him so we can *all* get a good night's sleep.' She winked at the girl.

The little band of friends said goodbye to Muriel and Elman and left the library. They were about to take the stairs when Aldiss stopped them. 'Wait!' he shouted. 'Look at this!'

Morag turned to see him pointing to a fat red button sticking out of the whitewashed wall. In bold black letters was the word: DOWN.

'What is it?' she asked.

'It's probably to activate the Moonstones in the ceiling,' replied the dodo dryly.

'No! No!' said the rat jumping up and down with excitement. 'It's not for that. It's a *lift* button.'

'Do you mean she made us climb all those stairs for nothing?' rasped the dragon. She bared her teeth and made Bertie flap in fright.

'Press it Morag,' Aldiss urged. 'You're bigger than me, you can reach it.'

'But there aren't any lift doors on the wall. Actually there's nothing here that even looks like a lift,' Morag said.

'Just do it!' Aldiss urged.

With a nervous forefinger she pressed the big red button. At first nothing happened, but then, from somewhere inside the walls, there came the faint sound of clanking, as if some very old machinery that wasn't used often had suddenly creaked into life. Grinding, grinding, and then...

'Oh!' gasped Morag, astonished. 'How did that happen?'

The wall had opened up to reveal a dark rectangular space. A blast of warm, stale air rushed up the shaft and blew over them.

'Welcome,' cooed a disembodied female voice from within. 'This is Rosemary, your elevator operator. Please wipe your feet and step inside.'

Morag looked at her friends. 'There's nothing in there to step on to,' she pointed out.

'I *said* step inside!' the voice snapped. 'What? Do you think I have time to wait about for you all day? Please step inside *immediately*.'

'But...' Morag began.

'It's perfectly safe,' Aldiss assured her. 'It's an old-fashioned Air Elevator. You're held up by an enchanted draught. Look, I'll go first and you lot can follow.'

Before anyone could stop him, Aldiss scampered over to the doorway and with a 'Geronimo!' dived into the dark chasm. When he fell into nothing he realised the 'enchanted draught' was missing. 'Eeeeeeeeeeeeeeee!' he screamed as he plummeted into the murky shadows.

'Bother!' said the lift, sounding surprised. 'I wasn't ready. Hold on sir, hold on!'

There was a creaking and groaning as the air came on and the screaming stopped. Then there was silence. Morag looked over the edge. She could see nothing, only the sort of darkness that made you think you had lost your sight.

'Aldiss?' she shouted, her voice echoing down the chamber. 'Aldiss? Are you all right? Aldiss? Answer me! Have you hurt yourself?'

'No, no bones broken...' Aldiss called back. 'No thanks to Rosemary!'

'I'm sorry sir. If you had only given me a bit of warning...' retorted the lift.

'Warning? You're supposed to be ready all the time.'

Morag rolled her eyes and turned to speak to Shona and Bertie, but found them gone. They were ten stairs down when she called after them.

'Where are you going? Aren't you taking the lift?'

'After that? I'd rather try and fly!' the dodo answered, plodding down the stairs two at a time.

'We'll see you at the bottom,' said the dragon bounding after him, her great green tail snaking behind.

'Well,' Morag said to herself. 'Nothing ventured, nothing gained.' She strode over and shouted: 'Get ready, Rosemary!' With tightly-shut eyes, she launched herself into the lift shaft, and into a fierce gust of balmy air.

'Going down!' called Rosemary cheerfully as Morag watched the doorway speed away from her. Faster and faster she fell, until she thought the skin was going to be blown from her face and her hair ripped out at the roots. The tails of her open duffel coat flew behind her like a woolly red parachute. She jolted to a sudden halt in mid-air. In the darkness, she could see nothing, hear nothing and smell nothing except for the faint odour of fresh grease.

There was a blink of light. A Moonstone switched on, filling the narrow lift-shaft with a soft blue haze. Morag felt herself being gently set down on the floor, as a door opened to reveal Aldiss waiting for her. His little furry face broke into a wide grin when he saw her, revealing a set of huge yellow teeth.

'Wow!' she laughed as she stepped out. 'That was amazing!'

'Let's do it again!' he cried excitedly.

'There will be plenty of time for that later,' said another voice firmly.

They turned to see Bertie on the stairs, followed by Shona.

'Come on, we've got work to do,' added the dragon. 'Montgomery needs to be told about the missing tooth. And fast!'

chapter four

Montgomery lived in a large house surrounded by high hedges and acres of grassland on the edge of Marnoch Mor. Its solitary position gave him the privacy he needed for his 'research'. What that involved was a mystery to everyone but Montgomery, and that was how he liked it. Set back from the road, the house's red tiled roof was all that was visible from the front gate where Morag, Bertie, Aldiss and Shona now found themselves. The gate was as tall as a double-decker bus and cast from silver from the Denebola star—according to Bertie. It had been shaped by a master silversmith into intricate swirling patterns that, the dodo informed them, depicted the four elements: water, fire, earth and wind.

'All very nice,' said the dragon, 'but where's the doorbell?'

'Is this it?' asked Morag pointing to a large chain. Without waiting for an answer she pulled it, and somewhere far away a horn sounded.

'Who is it?' a voice from the gate asked.

They looked at each other.

'I said, 'who is it?'' the gate asked again, this time impatiently.

'Er...it's Morag with Shona, Bertie and Aldiss,' replied Morag uncertainly.

'State your business.'

'We're here to see Montgomery,' the girl said.

There was a pause. 'Stand forward one at a time so that I may scan you.'

'Scan us?' repeated Morag.

It was a thought that rattled around everyone's head at the same time and no-one was keen to go first. They were even less enthusiastic when a robin decided to take matters into its own wings. It flew straight at the panel depicting fire. There was a *Zimm!* as it lit up and *Zap!* The little bird was fried mid-flight. The smell of burnt feathers filled the air.

'Interloper!' spat the gate. 'Now, step forward. I need to verify who you are.'

Morag looked in horror at Shona who had turned a sickly colour of purple (dragons turn purple when they're nauseous). Aldiss and Bertie were fairing no better: the rat was standing close by breathing deeply and the dodo was staring, his beak open in horror.

'You first, Bertie,' said Aldiss, pushing him forward.

'But it doesn't like birds,' replied the dodo, resisting. 'Why don't *you* go first? You're the littlest.'

'That is exactly why I should go second. What if it can't scan me? What if it frazzles me too, like that poor little bird,' said the rat, his black eyes filling with tears.

'And what about *this* poor little bird? Don't you care about *me*? There aren't many dodos left you know...' snorted Bertie, pointing at himself.

'Oh for goodness sake will you two be quiet?' interrupted Morag. '*I'll* go first, okay? And I'll be fine.' *I hope*, she thought as she moved towards the gate.

'No Morag, you can't!' said Shona, leaping in her way.

'I can and I will. We need to see Montgomery and we need to see him now,' she said firmly. 'Besides,' she added, 'it's freezing and it looks like it's about to snow. If you want to stay here and turn into an icicle that's fine but I'm going in.'

As she said this, a flurry of snowflakes fell and swirled around them. The dragon, seeing Morag was right, nodded her head.

'I'm ready,' Morag said, her stomach churning with fear.

'Come closer,' the gate replied. 'So I can see how you measure up.'

Morag moved closer and was engulfed in a funnel of light filled with thousands of sparkling shapes. As she looked closely, she saw that these were tiny star-shaped elves. They were taking out little measuring tapes and holding them against her.

'Morag MacTavish from Irvine, blue eyes, brown hair and a sharp mind,' said the gate. 'You're rubbish at telling jokes and your favourite food is macaroni cheese. You are the vanquisher of the warlock Devlish and saviour of the Eye of Lornish. Your biggest fears are meeting Mephista again and being found by your guardians Jermy and Moira Stoker. You may pass through.'

Astonished, Morag stepped out of the light and through the open gates. She waved to her friends from the other side. Aldiss went next.

'Cheese lover,' decided the gate. 'Collector of antique miniature thimbles. Karaoke singer. Vintage train enthusiast.'

Then Bertie.

'Pompous! Lover of television soap operas and gossip magazines. Only bird to have finished the Toughie Crossword in the *Marnoch Mor Herald*.'

And finally Shona.

'Bad tempered but quite loveable. Enthusiastic pickle eater. Secret writer of romantic novels.'

'Antique thimbles?' said Bertie.

'Soap operas?' replied Aldiss.

'*Romantic novels?!*' both laughed as a bashful Shona stepped out of the light. She coughed, 'Well, I wouldn't call them *romantic* exactly. Yes, they explore dragon-feelings and dragons in love but they're really all about...' She broke off when she noticed no-one was listening. Morag, Bertie and Aldiss were already running ahead up the driveway.

It had been extremely cold for days and the ground was still frozen underfoot, causing them to slip and slide. Red-faced, they drew breath before Morag climbed the big stone steps to the red front door and rang the bell. Ding-a-ling-a-ling, it chimed. She turned to her friends and smiled. Any minute now someone would appear.

Nothing.

Ding-a-ling-a-ling. Morag rang the bell again. Several minutes passed and still there was no response.

'Must be the housekeeper's day off,' said Shona.

'Let's go in anyway,' Morag suggested. 'We can't wait about outside all day. Montgomery's probably in his study and can't hear us.'

'We can't do that!' Bertie said. 'It's rude to go into someone's house without an invitation.'

'This is no time to stand on ceremony,' said Shona pushing past him. The door swung open to reveal a darkened hallway.

'Hello?' called Morag as she and the dragon stepped inside. 'Anyone home? Montgomery? It's me, Morag! And Shona and Bertie and Aldiss. Is it all right if we come in?'

She looked at the others then peered inside again. The house was deathly quiet. Such a large house would normally have at least a housekeeper and maybe even a gardener, but there was no-one in sight. Not even the owner, who was always at home at this time of day.

'Montgomery? It's quite important,' the girl called.

'He must be in his study,' the dodo. 'I'll show you the way. I've been there before. Many, many times.'

Morag rolled her eyes. The hallway was long, oak panelled and decorated with spears and bows and other armoury of the sort you would see in an old castle. A couple of deer antlers hung from the wall. Above the staircase hung a tapestry depicting the founding of Marnoch Mor. Morag recognised Colm Breck in it, but was unsure of the others. One was a pale, dangerous-looking red-haired man. He seemed familiar. She assumed the woman wearing the crown must have been the town's first monarch, Queen Adela Augusta. In the background, the face of another man stared out. He looked like…Montgomery! Morag frowned. *Why would he have been put in the tapestry?* She wondered. *He couldn't have been around hundreds of years ago.* She didn't have time to muse over it, for her attention was caught by her friends.

'Where *is* the study, Bertie?' asked Aldiss impatiently.

'Er…down this corridor, I think,' replied the bird pointing. With his beak he opened a door that revealed a passage leading to the back of the house. 'Follow me!' he called. 'This way!'

There was only one door at the other end and it opened into a large, well-lit room with huge arched windows and bookcases covering three walls. Morag noticed what smelt like rotten eggs, but said nothing because she started in surprise. Montgomery was leaning against his oak desk in the middle of the room. He did not seem to hear or see them. He was staring at the ceiling above his head.

'Montgomery?' Morag ventured.

'Excuse me, sir?' tried Bertie.

Montgomery did not respond; he did not even move.

'What's he looking at?' whispered Aldiss.

'There's nothing there,' replied Shona looking up. 'Oh…wait a minute…what's that?'

A dark spot was spreading on the ceiling directly above the wizard. As they watched, it grew into a cone of swirling air, a tornado which spun furiously, scattering all the papers and books from the desk. It seemed to scream at Montgomery but he was rooted to the spot.

'Look out!' cried Morag, her hair whipping around her face. Too late. The tornado exploded and with an audible gulp, swallowed the wizard. The last they saw of him were the soles of his shoes disappearing into the vortex. Morag jumped to try and catch him, but just as she did the whirlwind gave out a final groan and disappeared altogether.

'MONTGOMERY!' she screamed.

But there was only silence.

'What *was* that?' Morag wept. 'Where did he go?'

'Could it have been one of his experiments?' asked Aldiss.

'Absolutely not,' said Bertie. 'He would never try anything that dangerous. In all my years as a trainee wizard I've never seen anything like it...'

'Now what?' said Morag.

There didn't seem anything to say or do but stand and look at each other in total despair. *Now what?* That phrase rattled around Morag's head like a captured wasp in a jar. She looked at each of her friends and saw reflected in their faces the same terrible turmoil that she felt.

'Oooh!' A soft groaning rose from the floor behind the desk. 'Ooooh!'

Morag looked at Shona whose ears were twitching to catch the sound again. 'Did you hear that?' said Morag, peering round to the other side of the desk. 'It sounded like someone was moaning, but there's no-one here.'

'Ooooooooh!'

She got down on her hands and knees and placed her head on the floor to look under the desk. At first, she could see nothing in the tight dark space between the bottom drawer and the rug. Then something glinted at her. She jammed her hand under and reached for it.

'Nnnggeuh! Can't...quite...reach it!'

The back of her hand screamed with pain as she shoved it further under, fingers outstretched. The tips just touched a smooth, shiny thing and with a nail, she drew it towards her. She pulled out a long chain with a large gold medallion at the end of it.

'Henry!' she cried happily.

'What were you doing down there?' asked Aldiss.

'Aren't you normally around Montgomery's neck?' asked Bertie.

'Do you know what's happened to him?' asked Shona.

The face on the medallion flinched at all their questions and his little eyes remained closed. 'Will you all stop shouting at me for a moment and give me time to recover?' Henry snapped. 'I have a terrible headache. For goodness sake be quiet, will you?' Everyone held their breath. At last Henry opened his eyes and looked around. 'Did you see what happened?' he said, addressing Morag. She took a breath before explaining how they had found Montgomery motionless before he was swept into the whirlwind.

'There was nothing we could do,' she added.

'A whirlwind?' said the medallion, face set in concentration. 'The last I remember was that I was round Montgomery's neck. We were looking through an old spell book together. Monty wanted my opinion on something he had found there. Then we heard something odd—'

'What did you hear?' asked the dragon.

'Well if you'll let me talk, I'll tell you,' replied Henry irritably. 'It was a strange barking laugh. It came from the ceiling. And when we looked up there was a blinding flash and Montgomery stopped moving. It felt like they used some sort of immobilising spell. That would certainly explain the flash...'

'They?' Bertie asked. 'There was more than one?'

'I never actually saw anyone, but I'm assuming it wasn't just a single person. Things happened so quickly.' He paused to reflect.

'So if they froze Montgomery, how did you get away?' the rat asked. 'Why weren't you affected by the spell?'

'It takes a lot to catch me out,' said the medallion haughtily. 'As soon as I realised what was happening, I unfastened myself and dropped. Just as well, because it just missed me.'

'It?' Bertie asked.

'Whatever it was that took him! Pay attention bird, will you? You're obviously losing the thread of what I'm trying to tell you!' growled Henry. 'I didn't see what it was, I was too busy escaping. I must have been knocked out when I rolled under the desk because I don't remember anything else until just now.'

'So you left Montgomery to face it on his own?' said Morag quietly. There was a silence as everyone took this in. The medallion suddenly seemed uncomfortable.

'Well, I wouldn't put it *exactly* like that...' he stuttered. He looked away, unable to meet her gaze. 'I thought I'd be more help to him here than wherever they were taking him.'

Morag sighed deeply. 'You mean you were too busy saving yourself to help him,' she said coldly. She pursed her lips and tried hard to keep the anger out of her voice. 'You might have been able to help him escape or...or...or at least keep him company so that he wouldn't feel frightened and alone,' she added, remembering when she had been taken to Murst as a slave two months before. Henry had been with her then and she had been very grateful for his friendship.

'I didn't think,' the medallion admitted, 'I just reacted.'

Morag snorted in disgust and the others looked away.

'Let's not get upset,' said Shona, breaking the uncomfortable silence. 'Standing around here arguing is not going to bring Montgomery back. We must search for clues. Let's do everything we can to find out who did this and why.'

'What do you suggest?' asked Bertie, flapping his wings in agitation.

'We need a rescue plan,' said Morag quickly.

Sitting on the leather chairs, the friends were able to establish three definite facts: Morag had been having recurring dreams about a ghost from Murst; Mina's tooth had been stolen and they believed a Klapp demon (creatures that are only found on Murst) was involved; and someone had kidnapped Montgomery from his own home.

It was obvious where they should start looking, for two of the three had links to the DarkIsle, Murst.

'What if all three are somehow connected?' Morag suggested.

'That would make sense,' said Bertie, and he told them about all the objects that had vanished from the human museums recently. 'On their own they may not seem significant, but if brought together they *could* be used for magical purposes. What I can't understand is why they also took Montgomery? What use is he to them?'

'Maybe they need someone to cast a special spell?' suggested the rat.

'Don't be so stupid, rodent!' snapped Henry. 'They must have used extremely powerful magic to get through the protection of the Eye in the first place. No mere novice witch or wizard could ever hope to achieve that. No, whoever has taken him must be very accomplished in magic.'

'Maybe they are going to hold him to ransom?' said Shona.

'But why?' Morag replied. 'What's unique about Montgomery, apart from him being in charge of the WWWC?'

They looked at each other, but no-one could come up with anything.

'He was here at the beginning,' Henry said quietly. 'Maybe that has something to do with it.'

'At the beginning of what?' asked Morag.

'He is the last of the ancient Founders of Marnoch Mor,' the medallion told the astonished friends.

'But that was 350 years ago!' Bertie spluttered. 'Montgomery can't be more than about 35. He's too young to have been one of the Founders.'

'He's 365 years old,' said the medallion. 'He doesn't like people to know in case they treat him differently.'

'But how is that possible? No-one else from that time has survived,' said a puzzled Morag.

'He has a unique connection to the Eye of Lornish,' explained Henry. 'It keeps him alive. He keeps it alive. One cannot do without the other for long.'

'Why didn't we know about this before?' Shona demanded.

The medallion's lips pursed and he frowned.

'It's hardly the type of thing one broadcasts to the whole world, is it?' he said crossly. 'If the information got into the wrong hands, someone might try to kill him or take the Eye. Marnoch Mor would always be vulnerable to attack, its streets would crumble and its people would die.'

'But someone *did* take the Eye,' Morag blurted out. 'We got it back, remember?'

'Yes and why do you think Montgomery was so keen to get it back that time? It was because the whole future of this kingdom—and his life—depended on it.'

'Oh my goodness!' yelped Aldiss. 'What you're saying is now that Montgomery is gone, it's not just his life that's in danger, but…'

'Marnoch Mor as well!' Morag finished. 'If we don't find him soon the whole of Marnoch Mor will be destroyed.'

chapter five

There was nothing else for it: they would have to return to Murst, a prospect none of them were relishing.

Bertie, knowing that they didn't have any solid evidence that the folk of the DarkIsle were involved, argued against it, but he was swiftly talked down by Morag and Shona. They were convinced the answers about the wizard's disappearance, the theft of the tooth and Morag's nightmares would all be found on the island.

'We don't have any other leads, Bertie,' said Morag.

The dodo eventually accepted this and agreed to go, but how were they going to get there? It wasn't like Murst was just next door. The island was hundreds of miles off the mainland and invisible to all but those who had been there.

'Let's get to the sea first,' suggested Morag.

'There are buses parked at the gates,' Aldiss put in. 'It'll be quicker over land to Oban and from there we can get Kyle the Fisherman to ferry us out to Murst again.'

'We can't hang around,' said Morag, placing Henry and his chain around her neck. 'Come on, let's go!'

She rushed towards the door, expecting everyone to follow, but was stopped in her tracks by Henry. 'Just a minute!' he shouted. 'There is a quicker way of getting to the gates than going through the town.'

Morag held Henry up to look at him. 'There is?'

'Only Montgomery and I know about it,' he said imperiously. 'So this is top secret. You must never tell anyone else. Do you all understand?' He looked around to see the nodding heads of the dragon, rat and the dodo. 'Morag, do you promise never to tell?'

'Of course I do. Just get us there so we can leave as soon as possible.'

'Now I want you to take me back to the desk,' the medallion instructed. 'Do you see that little statuette of the goddess Athena? Yes, that one. Pull it towards you.'

Morag, who hadn't noticed the little marble figurine before, placed her fingers on its head and flipped it towards her. There was a swoosh, and they spun round. A large trapdoor had opened in the floor below the windows, revealing the unnerving darkness of an underground passageway.

'This will take us down to the river!' said Henry gleefully. 'No time to waste gawping.'

Without another word, Morag rushed over to see a stone stairwell leading into the gloom and, urged on by the medallion, the girl began to descend.

'Did he say *river*?' shivered Aldiss as he followed Bertie.

'I think so,' the bird replied, carefully negotiating his claws on the cold hard steps.

'Does that mean there's water involved?' the rat could be heard saying as he disappeared into the inky blackness. His squeaky words echoed back up to the study. There was an audible sigh from the bird and their words became more distant and muffled.

'Wait for me!' called Shona, bounding over to the hole in the floor. She peered down nervously. The stairs seemed steep for a dragon of her size and there was no light. She crawled down the steps, her long green tail winding down after her. With a small *shoom*, the trapdoor closed behind her, plunging them all into total darkness.

The friends stumbled and stalled on the way down, unable to see where they were going. There were many cries of 'ouch!' and 'Get off my tail, will you?' before they reached the bottom. With her hand on the cold stone wall, Morag encouraged the others along a passageway.

At last, they saw a chink of light ahead. It grew as they walked towards it until they could see quite clearly. It was a doorway into another chamber, a doorway that was glowing with a bright green light. Morag approached it and found magical-looking symbols had been expertly etched into it.

'These are amazing. What do they mean?' she asked Henry, tracing the markings with her fingers.

'How should I know?' the medallion snorted. 'I can't know everything! Open the door, will you, I'm not enjoying this darkness.'

Deflated, Morag looked at her friends. *Go on*, their faces urged, so she placed her hand on the metal handle. It felt ice-cold and hard. 'Here goes.' She turned it and the door swung away from her. Without looking back, Morag stepped inside. 'Oh my goodness!' she said. The others jostled in behind her. They were standing on a broad stone ledge over a canal in a dim cave. Moonstones in the ceiling sent shadows across the water, which glowed blue and clear. Moored to the ledge was a wooden dinghy bobbing below them.

'To the boat,' Henry ordered. 'Hurry, we don't have much time.'

Morag jumped in first, followed by Bertie and Aldiss. They had to hold on as the boat rocked dangerously when Shona climbed aboard, almost tipping them out into the water.

Brrrrring! came a noise from the stern. They all looked round to see that a green elf with webbed feet had appeared. He was munching on a huge sandwich.

'Behold!' said the elf wearily between bites. 'I am the Whitewater Boatkeeper. Or the Elf of the Punt. Whichever you like. Where to?'

'Can you take us to the town gates?' Bertie asked. 'We shall be most grateful,' he added when the elf frowned at him.

'And what shall be my payment, guv'nor?' the

creature said, casually flicking a lettuce leaf into the water.

'How about a sandwich of your choice, oh elf person!' Bertie replied.

'*Anything* I like?' the elf asked. He eyed the dodo suspiciously. Bertie nodded.

'Nice try,' the little man said. 'But I don't smell bread on any of you.'

Bertie patted his magic satchel. 'This bag can produce anything I ask for. Test me!'

'It'll cost you a pickled Orlan fish with Brussels sprouts and marshmallow sandwich,' said the elf. He waited for the dodo's reaction.

'Consider it done!' said Bertie, triumphantly removing a steaming, gold-crusted sandwich dripping with melted marshmallows. 'Now please, let's get going.'

The elf grabbed it and tucked in into his short green jacket. Without another word, he leapt onto the ledge and untied the mooring ropes. Giving the boat a nudge from the shore, he leapt back on board and took hold of the rudder. Aldiss leapt to the bow. 'Charge!' he squeaked, whipping his tail excitedly.

The boat began to drift leisurely down the canal.

'I thought you said this was the *quick* way?' Morag hissed to Henry. The medallion harrumphed. 'It ought to be. Point me to him,' he ordered. Morag swivelled round in her seat and held up the medallion. 'Boatkeeper, can you please increase the speed,' said Henry. 'We can't waste time. We must reach the gates quickly.'

'Ah, what's the hurry?' grumbled the elf.

'A friend's life depends on it,' said Shona.

'The express service will cost you another sandwich.'

'Now wait a minute! That's not fair,' flapped Bertie.

'Ooooooh!' replied the elf theatrically. 'Well, maybe I like to take things slow and maybe I'll just keep going at this speed and maybe you'll just have to lump it. Unless your little magic bag has something else in there for me...'

Before Bertie could answer, Morag stepped in. 'Didn't you hear what the dragon said? Our friend's life is in danger. Now unless you want yours to be in danger too you'd better step on it!'

The elf looked Morag up and down, his eyes wide with surprise. He could see she meant what she said. 'Hold on tight!' he said. He let go of the rudder and swung his legs out of the boat and into the water, then he began to paddle with all his might. The boat ploughed forward, faster and faster, until the walls and the canal became a long blur of blue-grey. Seconds later they arrived, with a lurch and a huge spray of water, at another dock.

'This is the nearest port to the gate,' the elf informed them as he climbed back into the boat and gave his dripping feet a shake.

'Thank you,' said Morag jumping off onto the

stone floor. The elf gave her a quick nod. Once all of his passengers had disembarked, he swung the boat out into the water again and sailed off down into the tunnel, singing loudly between bites of his hard-earned sandwich.

'*He* was a strange little man,' Morag remarked as the elf's voice was finally swallowed up in the darkness.

'All Whitewater Elves are like that,' Bertie replied. 'They're a peculiar lot. Only live for the fun of tearing down fast rivers. Can't understand what that one is doing here. I wouldn't have thought it was his sort of place.'

'He was banished,' replied Henry from Morag's neck. Before they could ask any more questions he added, 'Now can we stop jabbering and get on?'

A stairwell rose from the dock in a tight spiral, reminding Morag of stairs in a castle tower. They climbed until they came to a trapdoor in a low ceiling. Morag placed both hands against it and pushed, but it did not move. Bertie and Aldiss ran to help her and together they pushed some more.

'Let me try,' said Shona.

It was a tight squeeze, but somehow Morag, Bertie and Aldiss got out of the way to let the dragon past. She put her great green shoulder against the trapdoor and...

'Nggghhhhh!' She shoved with all her dragon-might. 'Oh this is no use! Stand back and cover your heads for this bit.'

Unsure of what she planned, Morag, Aldiss and Bertie jumped down a few stairs and ducked. Shona inhaled deeply and blew a blast of fire from her mouth, the flames licking greedily at the old wood. After a few seconds of white heat, the trapdoor creaked, buckled and disintegrated, leaving behind a smoking pile of cinders.

'Told you I'd get it open,' Shona smiled as she cleared the remnants of the door and climbed into the chamber above.

One by one they clambered up and found themselves in what appeared to be the cellar of a pub. There were large barrels of ale lined against one wall; another had shelves filled with packets of 'Snap Crack Cauldron-Boiled' crisps and tiny bottles of 'Human Style' soda; a third wall was propped up with wine racks and beer bottles; and the fourth was empty save for a wooden stair-case leading upwards. Without a word to each other, they climbed it and opened the door at the top. Morag glanced out. 'I'm not sure where we are,' she said.

'Let *me* have a look,' said Aldiss. He peered out then smiled. 'We're in the Gallipot Inn at the bottom of Merlin's Walk. We're minutes from the gates. Come on.'

Before they could stop him, Aldiss threw open the door and scurried past the astonished faces of the handful of customers and an indignant barman. Sheepishly, the others followed and skipped outside into the cold winter's day before anyone could ask why they had been in the cellar. Morag pulled the door shut behind her just as the barman shouted: 'Hoi!' They raced down the street and round the corner, all panting hard. They stopped and gathered their breath.

'There's the gates!' they heard Aldiss shout excitedly.

'Aldiss! Wait for us!' Bertie called as he waddled after him, face red with exertion. But the rat was already hurtling towards them. Shona, Bertie and Morag could do nothing but follow.

When Marnoch Mor was built, a wall was erected around the kingdom to keep the townspeople safe inside. Over this a huge dome was created by the Eye of Lornish to make Marnoch Mor invisible to the outside world. The townspeople had always felt safe inside—until now.

As Morag ran after the rat, she realised the streets were full of worried people scurrying here and there as if the end of the world had come. She was so distracted that she did not look where she was going and ran flat into a gate guard. It sent her flying backwards onto the cobbles. She winced as she hit the ground, but the guard did not move and stood to attention.

'What are you doing here, Miss?' he said, as Bertie and Aldiss helped the winded girl to her feet.

'We need to leave Marnoch Mor,' she replied breathlessly. 'Please, will you open the gates for us?'

The guard sniffed and looked down his large

nose at her. 'Sorry, but I can't do that,' he said. His eyes snapped front again. 'They are locked until further notice.'

'You must let us out,' Shona said before Morag could get a word in. She stood close to the guard, staring at him intently. There was only one word for her manner towards him and that was intimidating.

'Can't,' he replied testily.

'You can,' she said, eyes glaring. 'As Marnoch Mor's Special Chief Constable I order you to open the gates!'

'I *can't!*' he said again, this time a little more forcefully. He glared back at her.

'If you don't then I will!' growled the dragon. She dug her claws into the thick wood and tried to prise the gates open, but they did not move. Then, as her astonished friends watched, the angry dragon pushed the guard out of the way and punched at the multi-coloured buttons on the control panel. Still the gates stayed closed.

'Just a minute!' protested the angry guard. 'Get away from there.'

'Look, *why* can't you open the gate?' Morag asked.

'Marnoch Mor has been shut down,' he said. 'All of us are locked in. And that means no-one goes in and no-one goes out. That's the way it is!'

'What do you mean 'locked in'?' snarled the dragon, turning on him. Her scaly brow was almost touching his. He ignored her and appealed to Morag. 'Miss, please ask your dragon to remove herself. I'm just carrying out orders from higher up.'

Morag glared at Shona and with a nod of her head, indicated for her to join Bertie and Aldiss. Turning back to the guard, she said in her most reasonable voice, 'Sorry about that. Now why has Marnoch Mor been shut down?'

'If someone interferes with the Eye, the security system goes into defence mode. It locks the gates and seals the invisible dome above us to keep out any villain who is trying to get in. And keep in any villain who is trying to get out! No-one can open them again except for Mr Montgomery. The last time it happened was when the Eye of Lornish was stolen.'

'That's all very reassuring,' squawked Bertie from the side. 'But the Eye of Lornish hasn't moved. Look—it's where it should be.'

Morag turned round and there, standing above all other buildings—and still in its place on a huge spike on top of the clock tower of the Town Hall—was the bright Eye of Lornish. As she watched, its normally steady light flickered like a candle about to go out. In her short time in Marnoch Mor, Morag had never known it to do anything but dazzle like a star. It had certainly never failed before, not even for a second. This was worrying.

'It's Montgomery...' she whispered, remembering what Henry had told her earlier about the pair being linked.

'Eh?' asked the guard.

'Oh nothing,' she replied. 'Thanks for your help anyway.'

She turned to the others. 'Bertie, how did you and Aldiss get out before?' she asked.

'Before?' the bird looked puzzled.

'When I first met you. You and Aldiss were trying to find the Eye of Lornish but you came up through a tunnel into my basement by mistake. How did you get out of Marnoch Mor then?'

The dodo looked at the rat and they both shook their heads. 'Aldiss and I took the Underground as far as possible, then tried to find our way along the old tunnels,' said Bertie. 'But *someone* got confused...'

'The Underground is the last thing to close after an emergency shut down to let in any approaching trains,' Henry piped up.

'And Montgomery was still here to keep everything going for a while after the Eye was stolen,' added Aldiss.

'Do you think the Underground will still be running this time?' Morag asked.

'If it is, we can't have much time left before it shuts down too,' said Shona.

'Well,' said Morag, 'there's only one way to find out. Let's go.'

chapter six

As news of the lockdown spread, the streets of Marnoch Mor filled with witches, kelpies and all manner of strange animals. They streamed like a swarm of bees to the town square, where they hoped someone would tell them what was going on. Morag, Bertie, Aldiss, and Shona were swept along on the tide of anxiety and fear.

Rumble, rumble, rumble.

The ground began to shake and shudder. Buildings rocked and buckled, chimneys toppled and slates fell from roofs like leaves from a tree. The people screamed and ran for cover as a large jagged crack tore up the middle of the street. As the rumbling grew louder and the shaking more violent, the crack raced towards Morag, Shona, Bertie and Aldiss, like a plough tearing through soil, spitting up cobblestones along its way. Barely able to stand, the horrified friends could only watch.

Then the rumbling stopped as abruptly as it had begun. The crack was halted and the earth was still. An eerie silence fell as everyone waited. Minutes passed and no-one moved.

'I think it's safe,' Morag whispered to Bertie, who was standing closest to her. The dodo, wide-eyed with fear, could only nod dumbly.

'We have to get to the station before another quake hits,' Shona said abruptly, causing Aldiss to squeak in fright. 'Everyone climb on my back. It'll be quicker if I carry you all there.'

'Good idea,' agreed Henry.

As Shona squatted, Morag climbed on first, followed by the dodo and the rat. The dragon heaved herself to her feet and began to walk. She allowed herself a few moments to get used to the additional weight of her friends then, spurred on by the dread of another tremor, she began to run; Morag and the others clung on for dear life.

Everywhere they went they ran into more townsfolk emerging from doorways. Initially, they seemed stunned by what had just happened, and were walking around dazed, staring at the vast chasm in the road. An oppressive sense of urgency hung in the air, an underlying panic fuelled by the rising dust from fallen masonry. Nymphs and dryads began to talk and cry, dwarfs began to shout and fairies to wring their hands as they all hurried to the town square. Soon unicorns, elves, witches and wizards joined them as they strode to the only place they knew they might find an answer: Marnoch Mor Town Hall.

Shona weaved between them, careful not to knock anyone over as she rushed to the station. However fast she wanted to go, it became clear she would have to slow down. For, as she sped round the corner into Breck Street, she ran straight into a huge crowd, all coming the other way.

Shona searched for a way through, but the square was so tightly-packed it was difficult to see how they could go on. Morag slipped from the dragon's back and squeezed in front, determined to push ahead.

Small for her age, Morag found it difficult to force a path through the crowd. At first, nobody seemed to hear her shouting 'Excuse me!' at the top of her voice, but she pressed on and gradually she and her friends made their way to the centre of the throng. Despite the squash, Morag found that if she stretched up on her tiptoes she could just make out the familiar shapes of the fountains and the statue of Colm Breck on its plinth. In the distance, at the far end of the square, the huge half moon window of the Central Station rose above the crowds.

'Keep going,' urged Henry as Morag stopped to allow a family of unicorns to squeeze past. 'We must get to the station.'

'I'm doing my best. It's not easy you know,' she replied tartly. 'It's going to take a bit of time to get through.'

'Did you say you're going to the station?' a voice said behind her.

She turned to see a red-haired female dwarf carrying an axe staring up at her.

'Yes, we need to get there as soon as possible.'

'No point in doing that,' the little woman said,

'the trains aren't running. It's like the rest of this place: shut down for no reason.'

Morag was just about to open her mouth to reply when a loud crackle of electricity and a deafening buzz swept above the gasping crowd. She covered her ears and gritted her teeth and was almost at the point where she thought she could take no more when it suddenly stopped.

'What was that?' she asked, but the dwarf had disappeared. Shona answered. 'The Eye of Lornish,' she said. 'It is failing.'

They looked up at the Town Hall's clock tower. At the top the Eye of Lornish was wavering and flickering...and going out. There were several screams, some dryads fainted and the centaurs reared in fright.

'My subjects!' a voice boomed over the hysteria. 'Please be calm. Panicking will only make matters worse.'

Morag peered over the pointed hats of the wizards in front of her. Although she could not see much, she could make out the glittering brilliance of a silver crown against the sandstone.

'It's the Queen,' she said to the others. 'Come on, if we push forward we might be able to reach her and tell her what's happened. Surely she'll know how we can get out of here?'

As Her Majesty continued to try to calm her subjects, Morag and the others made their way towards the steps. Shoving, squeezing and jostling, they fought their way through, ignoring loud tuts and bad-tempered grumblings.

Queen Flora was standing on the top of the stairs, her small, slim body framed by the huge doors of the Town Hall behind her. Older than she looked, Flora was known for her quiet wisdom and was a trusted and beloved leader.

Surrounded by guards holding back the crowd, the Queen did not at first hear or see Morag and her friends, despite them doing everything they could to attract her attention. They waved, they shouted and Shona held Morag up in the air, but she barely looked their way. The Queen, focussing on reassuring her people, continued to talk. Nothing the friends did alerted her to their presence.

'We're getting nowhere,' said Morag suddenly. 'We need to try something else.'

'What are you planning?' asked Henry. He gleamed brightly around her neck.

'Watch this,' she replied.

Morag waited for her chance. The Queen was responding to a question from an angry Cyclops and all eyes, including the guards', were on him. Now Morag could move. She threw herself on to her hands and knees and crawled between many pairs of legs, human-like and animal, to get to the front. Checking the nearest guard was still distracted, she scuttled forward and scrambled between his legs too. She jumped to her feet, and ran to the Queen.

'Your Majesty, I need to speak to you!' she said, tugging the Queen's sleeve. Flora instinctively pulled back, surprised at first, then puzzled. The guards leapt to defend her, but she held up a hand to stop them. She smiled when she saw the worried girl in the red duffel coat before her.

'Don't I recognise you?'

'Morag MacTavish, Your Highness,' the girl replied.

The Queen was startled. 'Ah yes. You were involved in the return of the Eye from the Isle of Murst weren't you?'

'I'm a friend of Montgomery. I need to talk to you. He's in desperate trouble.'

'Montgomery in trouble?' said the Queen, 'I find that hard to believe.' She looked down and saw Henry. 'What are you doing with his medallion? Where is Montgomery?'

'Please, Your Majesty, you must believe me,' the girl continued breathlessly, 'Montgomery is in danger!'

'She speaks the truth,' Henry said.

Fear passed momentarily over the face of the Queen before she regained her composure. 'Are you *with* anyone?' she asked, looking behind Morag. Morag nodded and indicated Shona, Bertie and Aldiss. The Queen immediately instructed the guard to let them through. 'Come!' she said, ushering them up the steps.

'We've no time, Your Majesty,' Morag told her. 'You need to get us out of Marnoch Mor. We think we know where Montgomery has been taken, but we can't go after him.'

'The borders around Marnoch Mor have been closed for a good reason, young lady. In any case, what would you expect me to do?'

'You're the Queen; you're a descendent of the town's founders, so you know Marnoch Mor as well as Montgomery. You must know of a way out. You're our only hope.'

'This is an impossible situation. I could be putting you in terrible danger by telling you this...' began the Queen. She paused for a moment. 'But yes, there is a way,' she muttered. 'It's been closed for a very long time. I'm not even sure you will be able to get through.'

'*Please* tell me,' said Morag.

'It'll be dangerous. That thing, well it has a life of its own...'

Morag grabbed her arms and looked into her eyes. 'Montgomery needs us. If we don't get to him in time there's no saying what they'll do to him.'

'Go to Central Station,' said the Queen, having decided to trust Morag. 'There's a photo booth...'

And that was as far as she got. A piercing scream from the crowd made the Queen turn and gasp. There was a horrible, clawing smell of sulphur in the air. Morag thought she recognised it earlier. She craned to see what the Queen was looking at and was horrified to see a tornado sweeping over the heads of a group of panicking witches. It darkened and swelled, its winds whirling and whipping, moaning loudly as it went.

'It's coming for us!' Aldiss squeaked and hid behind Bertie.

'What *is* that?' asked the Queen.

'It's the same thing that took Montgomery,' replied Morag. 'And it's heading this way. Come on, run!'

The whirlwind lunged at the Queen, who stood as if mesmerised, just as Montgomery had been. The swirling winds lashed her hair and dress.

'Run! Now!' screamed Morag, tugging the Queen's arm. Flora came to her senses and she and Morag leaped up the steps and threw themselves against the Town Hall doors. They pounded on the hard wood, screaming to be let in, but the doors remained closed. Morag turned and stared as the roaring vortex closed in on them. Something long and narrow was pointing up from inside. It looked like...it *was*...a dart gun! It was being aimed at Morag and Queen Flora. Eyes wide with fear, Morag could only watch as there was a loud puff and something shot towards Flora.

'Watch out!' Morag yelled as she spun to push the Queen out of the way, but it was too late. The tiny arrow hit its target, its green feathers vivid against the pale white of the Queen's neck. With a sigh, the monarch's eyes closed and she crumpled to the ground.

'Queen Flora!' Morag screamed, rushing to kneel beside her. 'Wake up! Please wake up!'

Overhead, the tornado gave out a terrible roar

and as quickly as it had arrived it swirled away to nothing.

Shona, Bertie and Aldiss ran forwards. Flora's eyes fluttered open and she smiled, but no words came from her dying lips, which had already begun to turn a ghastly shade of blue. She gave Morag a final pleading look before closing her eyes for the last time. The girl, sobbing loudly, knew instantly that the Queen of Marnoch Mor was dead. Numb with shock, Morag could only look to her friends for confirmation of what had just happened. Their faces said it all. Shona, Bertie and Aldiss were horrified. And they weren't the only ones. The news spread through the crowd in urgent whispers. 'The Queen has fallen...That human girl is with her...'

'What happened?' asked a guard, checking for a pulse. He hadn't been close enough to see the dart fly from the whirlwind.

'A blow gun,' Morag said quietly. 'It came from the wind. A dart killed her straight away. She didn't even have a chance to move.'

'Where did it hit her?' he asked.

'What do you mean? The dart's still there. Look!'

But when the guard examined the Queen's neck, there was no sign of the poisonous arrow. 'I can't see anything.'

'I saw it!' Morag cried. She turned to her friends. 'You all saw it, right?'

Bertie looked worried, Aldiss shook his head and Shona said nothing.

'We ran in the other direction,' Bertie said. 'We thought we could hide round the back of the building. I personally didn't see what happened to the Queen.'

'Me neither,' Aldiss confessed.

Shona merely shook her head. 'Sorry, Morag.'

'The whirlwind killed her...with a...with a... dart,' the girl stuttered, confused. '*I saw it!*'

Shona put a big arm around Morag's shoulders. 'I'm sure you did,' she said kindly, 'but there's no sign of it now. Come on, there's nothing we can do for the Queen, but we can still try and rescue Montgomery.' She helped Morag to her feet.

'And where do you think you're taking her?' the guard asked, lowering his pike. Aldiss drew back and hid behind Shona. 'This is a crime scene and this little human is our only suspect. She's not going anywhere.'

The dragon narrowed her yellow eyes and bared her teeth in a low, rumbling growl. 'Listen,' she snarled, 'I am the Special Chief Constable and I order you to get out of our way.'

The guard, unperturbed by the large angry dragon, stayed put. 'Her Majesty Queen Flora has just been assassinated,' he said, 'And whether you are the Special Chief Constable or not, you are not going to help our only suspect escape!'

'Morag would never harm anyone,' Bertie stated. 'Would you, Morag?'

'Of course she wouldn't,' Aldiss piped up. 'The only person she's ever killed is Devlish.'

Bertie covered his face with his wing in despair. There was a murmur as the information passed through the crowd. 'The Queen is dead,' they said. 'They've caught her killer. It was that girl who killed Devlish on Murst, the one they let in from the human world—she's the murderer. She conjured up the winds to hide her while she killed our beloved Queen Flora. Murderer! Murderer! Murderer!'

Dazed, Morag looked around her. She couldn't believe that anyone thought she had assassinated the Queen. I didn't do it, she wanted to scream, I didn't do it, but no words would come. She felt the pressure of Shona's claw on her shoulder as the dragon gently pushed her forward towards the guard, who was brandishing his ceremonial pike in their direction.

'Get out of our way!' the dragon snapped.

'Halt!' the guard said. 'In the name of our late Queen, I command you to stop!' His cries caught the attention of his fellow soldiers who immediately fell in beside him. They too lowered their weapons, ready for a fight.

'Very well, if this is how you want to play it!' Shona sighed. Still holding on to Morag's shoulder, she took a deep breath and...

'Wait a minute!' cried Henry. 'I have a better idea!'

Shona breathed out, sending a dark cloud of smoke into the air. 'Go on then!' she growled. 'Quickly.'

Morag looked down at the medallion hanging around her neck. She saw Henry screw up his tiny little face as if concentrating very hard and then his eyes opened again. 'There!' he said.

Nothing happened. Not at first. Then slowly the guards dropped their weapons and stood back, creating a corridor through their ranks. Behind the friends, the crowd also began to move and soon cleared a pathway.

'Now isn't that a better way of getting what we want rather than frying everyone?' the medallion asked smugly.

'Show off!' the dragon muttered, pushing Morag forward.

No-one stopped them as they walked towards the Central Station. No-one said a word. The square had fallen silent and although Morag was relieved there were no further shouts, the mood of the people unnerved her.

'What did you do to them?' she whispered to the medallion as she climbed the stairs leading up to the station.

'I stupefied them for a little while. It's like sending them to sleep while their eyes are still open,' Henry whispered back. 'It's one of my more amusing spells. I'll teach it to you some day. Now, get a move on because I can't hold them all like this forever.'

chapter seven

The station was deserted. With no-one to stop them, Bertie locked the doors behind them and they ran towards the platforms.

'Before she was killed, the Queen tried to tell me there was only one way out,' said Morag. 'Something about a photo booth.' She looked around frantically but could not see one.

Marnoch Mor Central Station was enormous. It was the hub of the Secret Underground railway: every track that secretly ran under the human world led here. There were at least forty upper platforms and more downstairs, according to the signs that floated in mid-air. Although arrows pointed in various directions, none gave any indication of where there might be a photo booth. Morag scanned the platforms and the abandoned engines sitting there. None of the trains moved, no-one got on or off, and nothing stirred. The stillness gave her the shivers.

Beside the platforms, the ticket offices, where bored ticket officers usually sat, were silent and empty. Above them, as black as a chalkboard on the first day of school, were the train information screens, but with no trains leaving or arriving, they were blank. Morag peered up to see if she could see the Battuns, the little bat-like creatures who drew and redrew the board, but even they had scattered.

She glanced at the market stalls nearby, offering 'Wand and Magic Crystal Repairs' and 'Human Costumes' (consisting of a father, mother and a child). Everyone must have fled with the first earth-tremor, tipping over one stall in their panic, and scattering bottles of enchantments and rainbow ribbons across the floor. It was the only thing in the station affected by the chaos outside; the other stalls had remained upright and intact—and abandoned.

'*Where* are the photo booths?' Morag cried in exasperation. 'Shouldn't they be where everyone can see them?'

'They are here somewhere,' Shona assured her. 'One of my volunteers used one only the other day.'

A low rumbling began outside and got steadily louder.

'Listen,' said Morag. 'What's that?'

'Do you think it's another tremor?' asked Aldiss, watching the floor as if he expected it to split open.

'It sounds different this time,' said Bertie. 'Like lots of people speaking at once.'

They heard a cry of 'Murder!' and then one of 'Vengeance!' and then 'Let's get her!'

'Oh dear,' said Henry. 'I think my spell's just worn off.'

Morag turned to Shona. 'We can't stay. They'll get in here in no time. Can you remember where the volunteer went?' she demanded. 'Did he say?'

Shona frowned. 'I...uh...hold on till I think about it. He said he came here and...'

'Excuse me!' squeaked Aldiss, tugging on Morag's coat.

'In a minute Aldiss, Shona's trying to remember,' the girl said.

Aldiss sighed, but would not be put off. 'I said, excuse me!'

'Not now!' snapped Morag who was feeling very frightened. People were already rattling the station doors. The rat, face pursed in annoyance, got a better hold of Morag's coat, hoisted himself up and scrambled up her arm. Before Morag could do anything about it, she found him sitting on her shoulder.

'It is over there!' he squeaked in her ear, tiny fingers pointing.

He climbed down and scampered in the direction of the toilets, wedged between the ticket booths and the entrance. His little paws skittered across the marble, echoing and distorting off the vaulted ceiling, so that instead of it sounding like one rodent, it became the noise of hundreds. Morag and the others watched as he slid to a halt at a white box that was almost invisible against the paleness of the station's walls.

'Is *this* what you're looking for?' he shouted as he threw back its curtain to reveal the inside of an ordinary-looking photo booth. Morag could see a blue plastic seat, a slot for money and even a camera.

'Well done, Aldiss,' she said, running to join him, 'and sorry I was so snappy.'

'That's okay,' replied the rat.

'When you've quite finished,' Henry groaned from around Morag's neck, 'perhaps we can get down to the business of rescuing Montgomery?'

Now the awakened mob was pounding on the doors.

'Come on, before they break them down,' said Bertie.

There seemed nothing strange or untoward about this photo booth. Morag walked around, looking it up and down, while Shona checked the roof.

'Why did Queen Flora send you to this thing?' Bertie asked.

'She started telling me there was an escape route out of Marnoch Mor when all the others had been closed,' Morag said. 'Perhaps there's a clue or a map inside.'

'I've already looked, but I couldn't see any-thing,' Bertie replied.

'Let me try.'

Morag stepped behind the curtain and sat down on the seat. She knew human photo booths took pictures, but had learned that nothing in Mar-noch Mor was necessarily what it seemed.

'Try pressing buttons,' the dragon suggested.

Morag quickly pressed every one she could see, but no instructions revealed themselves.

'This is hopeless,' she said and stood up to leave. 'I think the Queen must have made a mistake, there's nothing here.'

'You didn't put in any money,' Henry pointed out.

'We don't need our picture taken,' she replied. 'We don't have time.'

'Trust me,' the medallion said.

Morag hurriedly sat back down. There was a coin-slot just below the camera. Beside it was a sign saying 'Attention'. She was sure it hadn't been there before. As she stared at it, some black lettering appeared:

If you want your photo taken,
Three coins will make it waken.
If it's something else you're after,
Place a token in the rafter.

Morag screwed up her face, puzzled by this. She glanced up at the roof. There didn't seem to be any rafters. Bertie pulled back the curtain and stuck his beak in.

'I'm not sure what this means,' said Morag.

'A token? Hmmm,' said the dodo. 'What kind of token?'

Just then there came a violent crash. Morag, Bertie, Aldiss and Shona jumped in fright.

'What's happening?' Morag gasped and pulled

back the curtain to see Shona and Aldiss watching the front doors with widening eyes.

'Now, don't panic Morag...' Shona started.
'But...'

'They're using a battering ram!' Aldiss squeaked.

'Get in beside me and Bertie,' she said. 'Or they'll see you.'

Shona picked the rat up by his tail and tossed him in, then squeezed in herself as the girl and the dodo were pressed against the glass. Outside, the battering ram began smashing the doors, sending the sounds of breaking glass and splintering wood echoing through the empty station.

'Henry! Do you have any clue as to what this rhyme means?' Morag cried anxiously, her throat dry and tight. If medallions could shrug, then Henry would have raised his shoulders high. Instead, he just sighed and said that he didn't.

'A token could be something else,' said Bertie. 'A gift for example.'

'What sort of gift would a photo booth want?' Morag asked, voice wavering.

They all thought for a moment before Aldiss squeaked: 'What about some furniture polish for the stool or cleaning fluid for its lens?'

'It might work,' replied the dragon, 'Bertie, this is where we need your magic bag.'

The dodo nodded, rummaged in his satchel and pulled out two long bottles. One filled with a fizzy violet liquid was marked: *Wand Buff, the magical way to show your wand you love it.* The other, filled with green slime said: *Lorn-ish, the Magician's Favourite! Two drops and your glass will sparkle like the Magic Eye.* Morag placed them on a ledge near the ceiling.

'Tokens accepted,' a mechanical voice said from nowhere. 'Please select an option. I can dispense advice on love, money and magical enchantment. If it's an astrological query, I can calculate your birth chart and predict your coming week. Palms will not be read. Tea leaves and crystal balls are not accepted. I don't commune with the dead nor give horse racing tips. Please select an option.'

'No, no, it's none of those things,' began Morag. Beyond the curtain the banging got louder and the yells more insistent. 'Queen Flora sent us here,' she continued. 'I'm not sure why when we needed an escape route to save Montgomery...'

Bang, bang, BANG!!

'Only the Queen and Montgomery can authorise the *Drop Function,*' the voice stated.

'I don't know what that means. Please help, we must get out of Marnoch Mor. Montgomery's life is at stake.'

The voice of the booth paused as if it were weighing up what she had just said. Then a final loud bang echoed across the railway station and was followed by the sound of many feet clattering through the entrance. The crowd were charging towards them.

'Eek!' cried Aldiss, as Bertie slapped a wing over his whiskery face.

'Please!' squeaked Morag.

'Engaging Drop Function. Please ensure you have all your hand luggage. Look directly into the camera. Smile. And enjoy your journey.'

Four pairs of eyes looked into the lens. There was a whirr and then SNAP! The brightest blinding light any of them had ever seen. Morag threw up her arms to shield her eyes. As she did, the sound of the angry mob disappeared and was replaced by silence. She slowly lowered her arms.

'Oh my!' she said as she looked around.

'I think we've found our way out...' said Henry.

The walls of the photo booth had gone and they now stood in an earth tunnel dimly-lit by flickering oil lamps. The air was warm and still and smelled musty, as if the tunnel had not been used for a long time. Morag looked round to see the startled faces of Shona, Bertie and Aldiss peering into the gloom.

'Well,' said the dragon regaining her balance, 'that was certainly an odd way to travel.'

'I liked it!' squeaked Aldiss enthusiastically. 'When this is all over, I'm going back to do it all again.'

Even Henry, who was not normally sensitive to the thoughts of others, knew that at that moment Bertie was rolling his eyes in disapproval at the rat's words.

'Come,' said the bird, ruffling his tail feathers and ignoring the rat's high fives. 'We have to find the nearest way out of here. You never know what could be hiding in a place like this.'

'I think there's something over there,' Morag said pointing to a large shape under a dark sheet nearby.

The dodo scrunched his eyes to try and make out what it was. 'This is impossible,' he said, reaching into his bag. He pulled out four Moonstones and handed them round. 'Here, these should help us see better.'

Bertie pulled off the cover, sending up a choking cloud of dust and revealing the dirty black engine of an old-fashioned steam train. 'Speckled hens!' he squawked. 'Do you know what this is? Oh my goodness! I can't believe it! This is incredible!' He danced around the engine examining it from every angle.

'Calm down feather-face,' snapped the medallion from Morag's neck. 'Anyone would think you've just found a pot of gold.'

'I have...I mean *we* have!' replied the bird. His beady eyes shone. 'Morag,' he said whipping a chamois leather from his satchel, 'be a dear and clean the nameplate for me. I can't quite reach.'

Morag did as he asked.

'It *is* her!' the dodo said, his voice wavering. He turned to his friends and dreamily said: 'We've found her!'

'What is he going on about?' Shona growled.

'I think he's finally lost his marbles,' added the Aldiss. 'It's all that seed he eats. I told him it wasn't good for him.'

'*What* have we found Bertie?' Morag asked.

'This, my dear friends,' the bird announced breathlessly, 'is the long lost *Flying Horse*.'

They all looked at him blankly.

'Marnoch Mor's first steam train,' he prompted. They each shook their heads. They had never heard of it. 'Built in 1853 by Jonathan Clayslaps, master engineer and Head Wizard at the Academy of Arts, Magic and Other Stuff. The engine ran for more than a century until it disappeared.'

The dodo waited for a reaction. He expected them all to be as excited about it as he was, but Morag, Shona and Aldiss said nothing. It was Henry who spoke. 'Who cares?' he said grumpily.

'Does it work?' asked Aldiss. The bird shrugged his feathery shoulders.

'Will it get us out of here?' asked Morag.

Bertie began to stutter an answer, but was stopped by the medallion adding: 'We're on a rescue mission in case you haven't noticed! You're too busy waxing lyrical about some old piece of tin when Montgomery's probably being tortured as we speak.'

'It's not a piece of tin...' Bertie protested weakly, 'it's the *Flying Horse*.'

'Yes, well all I want to know is will it fly us out of here?' Henry growled.

Morag and Bertie ran towards the cab and climbed onto the footplate. As Shona and Aldiss waited in the cavern they examined the *Horse*.

The dodo pressed the controls, his face a puzzled frown.

'What do you think? Can you start it?' Morag asked after shooing Aldiss off again.

'I'm not sure,' Bertie replied, holding a Moonstone up to illuminate a little book on trains he had fetched from his bag. The book was called *How to Do Just About Anything: Train Drivers edition.* He sighed loudly as he tried to read the instructions. After a few minutes, he shoved it roughly into Morag's hands and said grumpily: 'I can't understand this. You have a go.'

He stomped to the back of the cab and slumped down. Morag glanced between the instructions in the book and the controls. *There must be some way to get this thing going,* she thought. As she was doing this, she didn't notice Bertie suddenly smile and scramble to his feet.

'I don't know why I hadn't thought of this before!' he squawked, causing her to jump. Frantically, he rummaged in his satchel.

'What do you mean?'

'This,' the bird said triumphantly. He pulled out a big jar of grey dust. A white label proclaimed: *Instant Driver, just add water.* Bertie unscrewed the cap and took a quick sniff inside. He sneezed and emptied the entire contents on the floor. He dipped his wing once again into the bag and pulled out a glass of water. Without pausing for breath, he tipped it over the dust and waited.

Morag held her breath.

'This'll never work,' said the medallion.

'Shhh,' scolded the girl.

They waited. And waited. By now, Shona and Aldiss were standing outside the driver's cab anxiously watching and willing the magic dust to do something.

'I told you this wouldn't work,' Henry began just as the dust, which was now a soggy pile of mush, started to crackle and pop and then to flash with bright sparks. As they watched, it began to take the shape of a man, grey skinned and wearing a grey boilersuit and driver's hat. With a series of puffs he inflated to the size of an adult. The crackling and sparking and puffing came to a stop and the train driver snapped into life. He looked at the friends and smiled. 'Afternoon,' he said politely. 'Where may I drive you?'

He placed his big grey hands on the controls and gave them a wiggle. The train whinnied with delight.

'Did that train just whinny?' Henry asked.

'I think so...' replied Morag.

But they didn't dwell on it too long for they could not take their eyes off the driver. He had a look in the firebox. It was empty. Before Morag could even say '*We need fuel*', coke suddenly appeared and with a flash, caught fire. The tender, where the fuel and water were kept, gurgled as it filled up. Morag knew from science lessons that the water was needed to create the steam that made it go. The driver fiddled about with the controls and the train, snorting and snuffling with excitement, chuffed into life. He turned to the friends.

'Tickets please,' he said.

'Oh. We don't have tickets,' Morag replied.

'Then I can't take you anywhere,' he said.

'But...' she began. And then she remembered. Morag felt in her pocket and pulled out her little red book. It looked almost black in the dull light. She opened it and fished out the ticket stub her parents had left inside the book. Trying not to think about what she was handing over, she passed it to the driver.

'Will this do?' she asked.

'Marnoch Mor Railways,' he read with a smile. 'Perfect!' He took it from her and stuck it in a slot on the wall. 'Where to?' he asked.

'Take us to Oban and don't spare the horses!' said Bertie.

The driver saluted, pressed some buttons and with a few puffs, the train began to chug forward.

'Wait for us!' Shona shouted as she and Aldiss tried to clamber on board.

As the locomotive rolled forwards, Shona grabbed Aldiss by the tail and tossed him on board. Squealing, the rat sailed through the air and landed with a bump. Shona swung herself on board just as the train ploughed into the tunnel.

'Whooo-hooo, this is fun!' squeaked Aldiss as he poked his head over the side, his ears streaming behind him.

'Fun, he says,' spat Henry. 'I'm glad someone's enjoying themselves. I wonder if Montgomery is having fun wherever he is. I very much doubt it.'

Morag said nothing, but her stomach churned as she thought of what might have happened to him. She could only hope that now they were moving they still had time to save him.

chapter eight

On and on the train sped, flying down the long dark tunnels of Marnoch Mor's Secret Underground. Hours passed and soon the friends grew bored. It would not have been so bad had the steam engine been pulling a comfortable carriage. Without one they had to ride in the engine-room. It was cold, it was chokingly dirty and it was uncomfortable. Most of all, it seemed as if their journey would never end.

Sick of the smell of coal-smoke, Morag sat sullenly on the cold metal floor, thinking of Montgomery. She was wrapped against the chill in her red duffel coat and had tucked a blanket—courtesy of Bertie's bag—tightly around her legs. Aldiss, always hungry, had ordered a plate of cheese and grapes from the satchel and sat munching them nearby. He offered to share, but Morag waved him away, explaining that she was too worried to eat anything. The dodo, fascinated by the train, stood at the Instant Driver's side marvelling at everything he did.

Up on the bunker, out of view and stretched over a knobbly pile of coal, Shona tried to plan what they would do when they arrived at Oban. They would have to find Kyle the Fisherman again. He was the only friendly human able to take them to Murst. Her stomach lurched when she thought of her homeland. She was the last dragon to be hatched and raised on the DarkIsle and she loved it still, but could not bear thinking of it under the control of the evil forces of Murst Castle. There was another problem: how to get on to the island without being seen. The DarkIsle rose out of the sea on a bed of perilous cliffs, with only one safe bay for boats to dock—and that was overlooked by Murst Castle. The only other way onto it was to climb the rock face on the western side; something the dragon was not keen on trying.

'That's a bridge we'll have to cross when we get to it,' she said to herself as she shifted to get comfortable.

'Did you say something, lizard?' a little tinny voice asked. It was Henry. He was snuggled up against the cold inside Morag's coat.

'Nothing that would interest you,' Shona replied sniffily.

'You said it,' the medallion retorted.

The dragon was about to say something back, when she was distracted by the train slowing down. It climbed up and out of the tunnel into the fresh open air and slowed to a halt at a familiar station. Morag scrambled to her feet as the arches of McCaig's Tower, a folly on a hill in Oban, came into view. Unaccustomed to the daylight after hours in the dark, she scrunched up her eyes to see the little building before them. The station sat in the middle of the folly and looked just as it had when she had first seen it less than three months before: a small, red-brick building with decorative wooden struts and a cheerfully-smoking chimney pot. It was like seeing an old friend again.

'Time to get off,' she called to the others as the *Horse* came to a hissing stop at the platform. As she leapt from the train, a large European Eagle Owl in a dark blue station master's uniform hurried over, blowing a silver whistle. On his lapel was a name badge which said he was called Mr Mozart. He peered at the girl with his huge orange eyes before launching into a torrent of angry words.

'You can't leave that train here,' the owl shrieked. 'I'm expecting the 3.15 at any moment and your vehicle is taking up valuable track space. Move it along now. Shoooo!'

'But we've only just arrived,' protested Morag, taken aback by his bad manners.

'We didn't mean to take up your space,' said Bertie. 'We'll move our train right now.'

'See that you dooooo,' snapped the owl before turning round and marching back to his office.

'Well,' said Shona, '*he* needs to learn some manners. Don't worry, Morag, I'll get the driver to move the *Horse* right now.'

But Morag wasn't listening. Her eye had been caught by a crumpled piece of paper lying on the grass nearby. She knew what it was even before she scooped it up and unravelled it. Staring back was an old picture of her in her school uniform above the words:

Have You Seen This Girl?

***Still missing: Morag MacTavish
Much loved foster daughter of
Moira and Jermy Stoker.***

***Substantial reward offered for any
information leading to her return.***

Moira and Jermy were supposed to be her guardians but they had made her cook and clean and shop and wait on them from morning until night every day. If she hadn't come across Bertie and Aldiss, who had taken a wrong turn and ended up in their basement, she would still be trapped with them. She had thought they were gone from her life forever, but now she knew they were still looking for her. That was not good. She felt sick.

'The Instant Driver is backing the train out now,' said Shona. 'So there shouldn't be any more problems...Morag? Are you all right?'

'It's them,' she said, pointing to the poster. 'Moira and Jermy. They're still after me. Oh Shona, what if they're here, watching me right now?'

'Oh, they'll never find you,' the dragon said.

'How could they? They don't even know you're here.'

But Morag was not so sure. '*Why* are they still looking for me?' she said. 'They didn't have a kind word for me when I lived with them and now they're offering a reward!' She knew they hadn't cared for her, so why were they making so much effort since she had run away?

Bertie, who had noticed Shona and Morag looking at the poster, tapped Morag on the shoulder and said: 'Rest assured Morag, we rescued you from them before and we're not about to let them steal you back. Now, let's be off down to the harbour. We have to find Kyle.'

***

The climb down from McCaig's Tower wasn't as treacherous as it had been the last time they were here. Then they had been forced to negotiate the steep path in the dark, but now, in the wintery light of late afternoon, it didn't take them long to stumble down the hillside.

Thinking there might be prying eyes around, Morag ran ahead and kept a look out for other humans. Aldiss, however, with his nose twitching in the cold winter air, sought a different foe. He sniffed and snorted for the tell-tale stench of Klapp demons: the ugly, hairy, stinking spies of Mephista. With their long arms and legs and strong fingers and toes, Klapp demons got about by clinging to the undersides of cars and other vehicles. They were the something you saw out of the corner of your eye, or the horrible smell that came from nowhere.

'Do you think Kyle will be here?' Morag asked Shona as they reached the bottom of the hill.

'I hope so,' sighed the dragon. 'There's no way to reach Murst without him.'

When they reached the road, Morag told Shona and Bertie that they had to part, at least for a short time. 'A dragon and a dodo can't walk around a human town,' she explained. 'There'd be uproar and we can't risk you being captured. Aldiss and I will go and find Kyle. You two hide.'

Bertie and Shona agreed to stay in the woods nearby until Morag returned. A couple of months ago, they were welcomed at Eleanor's Excellent Eatery nearby, where anyone from Marnoch Mor could go without drawing attention to themselves. But Eleanor had sold Morag to slave traders from Murst and tried to kill Shona, Bertie and Aldiss with a potion. The plan had backfired when Shona swatted the potion away with a tray, and it bounced back to the witch and killed her instead. There was no way they could return there, so they were forced to hide in the woods.

As Shona hunkered down into a patch of cold ferns with Bertie beside her, Morag scooped Aldiss up, placed him on her shoulder and waved to her friends. 'We'll be back as soon as we can,' she called.

The walk down to the harbour took less than half an hour. It was beginning to get dark, the sky turning grey and menacing, with a dampness in the air that warned of a storm. The streets were deserted as Morag walked towards the sea; only an elderly couple and their little dog braved the cold afternoon for a jaunt down the high street. They seemed not to notice Morag and the rat on her shoulder. Not that Morag minded; she was relieved no-one had stopped her or asked her what they were doing there. The Missing Person poster had jangled her nerves and she was terrified she would be recognised and returned to the Stoker's dingy guesthouse on Irvine Beach.

At the harbour wall, Morag and Aldiss stopped and scanned along the line of fishing boats bobbing gently in the water.

'I can't see Kyle,' Morag said. 'And his boat's not here, either. The *Sea Kelpie*'s not here.'

'Let's split up and search for him. With your eyes and my nose we're bound to find him,' Aldiss suggested. Morag nodded. The rat scuttled off in one direction while Morag went in the other.

It only took minutes to confirm that the boat was definitely not there.

'What are we going to do now?' Morag cried. 'If Kyle's gone there's no way to Murst. And if there's no way to Murst, there's no way to rescue Montgomery.'

Aldiss sat down on the freezing cold flagstones and shook his whiskers. He, too, was feeling dejected. Neither of them—nor even Henry who was still tucked inside Morag's coat—noticed a tall, dark man approach.

'And what are *you two* doing here?' said the gruff voice.

'What's it to you?' Aldiss answered rudely.

Morag looked up as the stranger began to laugh. 'Kyle!' she cried. 'We've been looking everywhere for you. We thought you weren't here.'

'Well,' said the fisherman, scratching his head, 'if I'm not here, I must be a ghost.' He patted himself as if checking to make sure he was real. 'Nope, I'm definitely here.'

Morag ran to hug him.

'Hoi!' called a tinny voice from inside her duffel coat. 'Watch it! You're squashing me.'

'Is that Henry I hear?' asked the fisherman with a grin.

Morag nodded and pulled the medallion out. His gold face was furrowed into a scowl as he looked at his friends laughing. 'I'm almost pure gold, you know,' he snapped, 'which means I'm easily bent out of shape.'

'I'm sorry, Henry,' said Morag softly. 'I'm just so pleased to see Kyle again.'

'So,' said Kyle, 'what brings you back to Oban?'

As Morag and Aldiss told him the terrible things that had happened in Marnoch Mor and how they suspected Montgomery was being held on Murst, he stroked his chin thoughtfully.

'The *Kelpie* is moored in a cove a few miles

north,' he told them. 'It won't take long to get up there in a taxi.'

'There's only one problem,' said Morag. 'How are we going to get Shona and Bertie there without anyone seeing them? '

'It won't be too long before the light starts to fade,' Kyle said. 'In which case I think I might just have a plan.'

***

Shona and Bertie were hiding behind a large hedge when the others found them. The dragon was shivering and the dodo's feathers were puffed up against the bitter winter cold.

The fisherman's plan was simple: he would walk on ahead and if he saw anyone coming he would wave his scarf to alert them. Morag was to walk with Shona, Bertie and Aldiss and keep an eye out for any cars or individuals approaching from behind. It was getting dark now, Kyle said, so it would be easier to get them to the boat unnoticed.

'It's also starting to rain,' the cold dragon chittered. 'Can't we get going now? I'm freezing.'

The journey to the outskirts of town should have taken no more than ten minutes, but because Shona and Bertie had to dive into the undergrowth every time someone passed, it took over half an hour. They broke into a run when they reached a road without bushes or trees that turned out of town and headed north.

Night closed in around them. As the streetlamps blinked on, eerie shadows were sent across the pavements. People turned on their house lights and drew their curtains, making Morag wish she was back home in Marnoch Mor. She pulled up her hood as the rain began to lash down.

'How much further?' Bertie complained. His claws were aching and he was tired of flapping into ditches or behind damp patches of ferns.

'I'm not sure,' Morag stuttered. 'Kyle said the *Kelpie* was nearby.'

'Yes, but what's Kyle's definition of 'nearby'?' Henry asked from under her coat.

'In no time we'll be safe and dry on the *Sea Kelpie* and on our way to Montgomery,' she told them.

Just then she heard Aldiss squeaking in fright. Morag looked up to see Kyle running back towards them. He looked panicked. Realising something had gone wrong, Morag acted fast.

'Hide! Quickly!' she instructed her friends.

Shona and Bertie dived into a small copse of trees just as the headlights of a large white van came into to view.

'It's the police…' Kyle panted.

The van drew up beside them. A policeman slid out and put on his hat. He strode purposefully towards them. 'It's a bit of a nasty night to be out with a young child, don't you think?' he asked Kyle.

'Yes, officer,' the fisherman replied. 'That's why me and my...er...daughter here are heading back to the boat. Don't want to keep her out too long in this. She'll catch a cold.'

The policeman stared intently at Morag. She looked away, afraid to catch his eye. What if he recognised her and forced her to go back to Jermy and Moira's?

'So where are you headed?' the policeman asked. 'I can't see any boat.' He searched the dark horizon of the sea as if expecting to see the *Kelpie* bobbing up and down there.

'It's moored a little way up the road,' Kyle answered, pointing in the direction the policeman had come. The policeman nodded. 'Can I offer you a lift?' he asked. 'I wouldn't want your daughter here to get any wetter.'

'No!' said Morag too quickly. Kyle threw her a warning glance. The speed of her answer had been suspicious.

'What she means,' he said with a smile, 'is 'no thank you'. We'd rather walk. We've...er...got this bet on, you see, that she'll get there before me. It's a game we play.'

The policeman eyed them both warily. 'All right,' he said, 'but mind and go straight home. There's supposed to be a storm tonight.'

'Thank you officer, we will,' Kyle replied. 'Come on Morag, let's get you home.'

The policeman flinched when he heard Morag's name, but said nothing as they headed up the road in the direction of the cove where the *Sea Kelpie* was moored. Morag turned round a few times to see if he was still watching them. Eventually, she saw him head back to his van. 'Good, he's going,' she said to Kyle, who also turned to look.

'No, he's not,' the fisherman said.

'What?'

The policeman was standing at the door of his vehicle talking into his radio. His eyes never left them.

'Kyle,' Morag said, stomach knotting with fear, 'I think he knows who I am.'

'Don't be silly,' he replied. 'How could he know that?'

'Because Jermy and Moira are still looking for me,' she began. 'For some reason, they want me back, and I don't think they'll stop till they find me. If they've told the police I'm missing or that I've been kidnapped, we could both be in a lot of trouble.'

Kyle knew by her worried expression that she was telling the truth.

'Keep walking,' he said, 'we might just get away with it.'

'What about Shona and Bertie?' a muffled voice sounded from beneath Morag's coat. The girl unbuttoned her duffel coat and pulled Henry out. 'We can't leave them in the undergrowth,' the medallion continued.

'They'll have to hide until the policeman leaves,'

said Kyle. 'We'll come back for them later. Right now, we have to get Morag out of here. Come on, run!'

Without looking back, the pair broke into a run, but just as they were about to turn the first corner they heard a shout behind them.

'Hoi! You two! Come back here, I want a word with you!' the policeman bellowed.

'Keep going. Pretend you don't hear him,' Kyle whispered to the terrified girl.

'Hoi!' the policeman called again.

They heard the engine start, the gears squeal and the van roar towards them. It stopped with a screech about a metre in front of them. The policeman jumped out, angry now. 'Did you two not hear me?' he demanded.

'Sorry Officer, is something wrong?' Kyle asked innocently. 'We were in too much of a hurry to get home.'

As the rain continued to pour, the policeman glared at Kyle.

'I can see why you were in a hurry,' he said. He pulled a crumpled paper out of a pocket and looked at it. Then he stared at Morag.

'Aren't you Morag MacTavish? Missing from Stoker's Bed and Breakfast, Irvine Beach, North Ayrshire?'

chapter nine

Morag didn't know what to say.

'I...eh...' she stuttered.

'No, she's not,' replied Kyle sharply. 'I told you before: she's my daughter and we need to get home.'

'You won't be going anywhere I'm afraid, sir. I'd like you both to come back to the station with me,' the policeman said firmly. 'Then we'll find out exactly who she is. Come on, in the van with both of you.'

He grabbed Morag's arm, but as he did, an angry female voice yelled: 'Get your hands off my friend!'

The policeman looked up disbelievingly as Shona glared down at him, her yellow eyes burning and her nostrils smoking.

'Unhand that girl,' Bertie demanded as he flapped to her side. Without thinking, the policeman did as he was told. 'You're a...And you're a...' His mouth opened and closed like a fish but he couldn't get the words out.

'A dragon and a dodo, yes, that's correct,' said Bertie tugging Morag.

'Not so fast,' growled the policeman as he grabbed Morag's shoulder again. 'You belong in a circus,' he told Shona, 'and this one belongs in a cell. She's coming with me.'

'No!' squealed Aldiss from the ground. 'You're not taking her!'

'A talking rat now,' said the policeman, 'well, that's a new one.'

'A talking rat with wand!' replied the rodent, fishing a little polished stick from his woollen hat. Dancing from foot to foot, he brandished it like a swordsman.

'Aldiss!' Bertie warned. 'Put that wand away. You'll have someone's eye out with it.'

The rat didn't seem to hear. 'Aldiss!' the dodo said again.

'Don't try and stop me, Bertie,' said Aldiss, his eyes bright with excitement as he waved the wand, 'I know what I'm doing. I won't let this man take Morag. No way can he have her. She's our friend...and...oh...oops!'

Before he could finish, a stream of multi-coloured sparkles flew from the toothpick-sized wand. A flurry of bubbles hit the policeman in the face. Their tickling caused him to sneeze, fall to his knees, then snort and hee-haw loudly.

Morag gasped and stared. 'Aldiss,' she said. 'You seem to have turned him into a donkey.'

'That wasn't quite what I had in mind for him,' the rat confessed.

'Change him back,' Morag demanded.

The rat looked a little shamefaced. 'I can't,' he said.

'Why not?'

'I've not got to that bit in my night class yet—you know, *undoing* spells. We're studying it next week. I could come back then?'

Morag took a deep breath.

'That just goes to show how stupid it is to teach rodents magic,' Henry put in.

'What's the difference between teaching a rat magic and teaching a necklace how to talk?' Shona said in Aldiss's defence.

'I am not a necklace, I am a magic medallion! An amulet specifically created to perform magic. That's the difference, my dear lizard friend,' Henry replied snippily. After a moment, he added, 'I suppose you'll want me to fix this.'

No-one said a word because no-one wanted the medallion to feel he had the upper hand, but just then the donkey policeman decided to bray again.

'Please fix this, Henry,' Morag asked. 'And can you make sure the poor policeman doesn't remember a thing of this? I don't want him telling everyone who and what he's seen tonight.'

And so it was that a perplexed policeman found himself standing in the rain on a remote stretch of Highland road with no knowledge of how he got there. He knew his name, he knew where he lived, he knew he was a policeman, but what he was doing standing in front of his van, so far out of town, he didn't know. He blinked a few times and had a look around. He must have stopped for some reason, but he didn't know why. He got back into his van and drove back to the station. He had decided it would be for the best if his colleagues never found out what had happened.

Up the hill and round the bend a bit, a girl with a gold medallion, a fisherman, a rat, a dodo and a dragon were running across scrubland to a windswept beach. Moored off-shore, and gleaming white against the dark grey winter's sky, a fishing boat called the *Sea Kelpie* rocked jauntily on the incoming tide. Morag suddenly felt apprehensive.

'Are you all right, Morag?' Shona wanted to know.

'Yes,' she replied. 'I'm just a bit cold, that's all.'

'We'll soon be on board and we'll get warmed up,' the dragon reassured her.

I wonder if Montgomery is feeling warm right now, Morag thought as she clambered into a rowing boat. *I wonder if he's feeling scared for his life, like I was when I was taken there.*

'We're coming for you, Montgomery,' she whispered, wiping away a tear, as they rowed out to the *Kelpie*.

'Did you say something, Morag?' Henry asked.

'No,' the girl hastily replied. 'It must have been the wind you heard.'

***

As the *Sea Kelpie* set sail, Morag, Henry, Bertie

and Aldiss warmed themselves in the cabin with bowls of steaming Whimsical Porridge (from Bertie's satchel) and discussed what they would do when they reached Murst. Kyle and Shona stood on the bridge with hot cups of cocoa and talked about the fisherman's father, whom Shona had rescued when he was a young man. All of them feared what was to happen next, though none of them voiced it.

Shona and Kyle took turns to stay up and keep the boat on course, while the others bunked down for the night: Morag on Kyle's bed, with Aldiss curled up beside her, and Bertie fast asleep on a small seat next to the galley.

Morag tried to sleep, but every time she closed her eyes she thought she felt the brush of skeletal fingers against her cheek, or saw the dead eyes of the warlock Devlish peering in through the portholes. She shuddered and pulled the blanket closer as the boat continued on its long journey west to the hidden island far out to sea.

It was morning before they reached their destination. Pale yellow light filtered through the portholes and woke an exhausted Morag. Slowly she opened her eyes and looked around her. Kyle's cabin was silent except for the gentle sounds of Bertie snoring, head tucked beneath a wing. She sat up, and nearly tipped Aldiss on to the floor. His frightened squeaks woke the dodo with a jolt and he leapt up, flapping his wings and squawking loudly.

The racket brought Shona to the door. She peered in. 'What's happening? Is everything all right down there?'

'Everything is fine,' Morag yawned. 'We just woke with a start. Are we nearly there?'

The dragon nodded. 'Murst is on the horizon. I've told Kyle to sail wide and go round to the west coast. That way no one in the castle will see us coming. I'm hoping the cliffs aren't as treacherous as I remember. That's the only way we'll get ashore.'

Morag caught the anxiety in her voice.

'Won't it be terribly dangerous trying to scale them?' Bertie spluttered.

Shona tried to change the subject: 'Well, now you are awake, featherface, you might as well make breakfast. Have a look in your bag for a jar of pickled gherkins. I'm famished.'

Morag, Bertie and Aldiss joined Shona and Kyle up on deck, and after they had eaten, they discussed their plan.

'The first problem is getting onto the island,' said Kyle. 'Those rocks would smash the boat to smithereens. So, I'm afraid you'll have to row ashore.'

Aldiss squeaked, frightened at the prospect.

'And once over the western rocks we have to go through the Deep Dark Wood,' said Shona.

'Until we reach Murst Castle,' said Bertie.

'We'll have to trick our way in, like last time,' said Morag.

'I don't think they'll fall for that again,' the dodo replied. 'Besides, even if we do get inside we have no idea where Montgomery is being held.'

Shona looked sombre. 'You remember how many turrets and secret chambers the castle has, Morag. Where do we start looking for him?'

'It's no use,' Aldiss sniffed. 'We'll just have to go home and leave him there.'

'We can't!' Morag said, her voice trembling. 'Montgomery wouldn't leave us there, so we're not doing that to him. There *must* be a way into the castle. We'll just have to find it when we get there. Let's worry about getting onto the island first and then we'll work out the next step. What do you say?'

She looked around at her friends, willing them to join her.

'She's right about Montgomery,' Henry said from around her neck. 'He would not leave anyone behind. Marnoch Mor is crumbling, and the only person who can stop it is locked up on the nastiest island in the world. We're the only ones who can help him. We cannot turn back now. I'm in.'

'Me too,' agreed the dragon.

'And me,' Kyle and Bertie said in unison.

All eyes fell on the rat. Aldiss flicked his tail uncomfortably and at first seemed unable to meet their gaze, but when he did finally look up, Morag could tell from his shining eyes that she had won him over.

'Let me at them!' he cried.

'In that case,' said the dragon, 'we'd best start getting ready.'

Morag slipped on her coat; Bertie slung his satchel across his shoulder and preened his tail feathers; Aldiss took a few moments to adjust his neon-pink pompom hat and clean the morning toast from his whiskers; Shona stretched her claws and gathered any bits of rope she could find on board.

'I thought we were close to Murst,' said Morag, looking out at the empty stretch of undulating grey sea.

'It's there all right,' said Shona, 'just give it a minute and then you'll see.'

They all watched the horizon, searching for the smallest sign of the DarkIsle. At first all they could see was the dark grey sea against a pale sky. Then an ominous shape loomed on the horizon.

'Morag, look!' gasped Aldiss. 'The DarkIsle!'

The sight took her breath away. There it was, where nothing had been before; the towering landmass that was spoken about in whispers by sailors and feared by magic folk. The DarkIsle of Murst. Morag knew the cliffs were dangerous but as the mist around the island cleared, the sight of them still gave her a shock. Miles of black, jagged rocks tore out of the foaming waters. They were breathtakingly beautiful and stomach-wrenchingly scary at the same time.

Aldiss whimpered as he looked up.

'Do we have to go up *that way?*' he whispered to Morag. 'Why can't we fly?'

She nodded. 'If only it were that simple.'

'Now, there's no way we can take the *Sea Kelpie* up to the island,' began Kyle. 'It's too dangerous.'

'So we're going in this,' Shona called briskly, as she pulled in the rowing boat they had been towing behind them all night.

After thanking Kyle, Morag helped Shona usher the others to the boat. The dragon held the boat still while they climbed in one-by-one. It was not easy, for the sea was rough close to the island and the little boat crashed against the *Kelpie* with alarming ferocity. Morag watched its sickening rise and fall, took a deep breath and launched herself towards it. Clatter, her feet hit the bottom, she overbalanced and fell onto her face. There was no time to check if anything was broken for as soon as she righted herself a furry brown object flew towards her. Shona had thrown Aldiss from the fishing boat and he sailed through the air, squealing with a mixture of fright and pleasure. Morag caught him just as he looked like he might overshoot into the steel grey sea. Bertie, with wings flapping furiously, followed and then it was Shona's turn.

She hung off the side of the *Kelpie* and put one leg out to reach the side of the bobbing boat, but the sea had other ideas and whipped it away from her.

'Bertie, Aldiss, you sit at the back to balance the boat,' said Morag. 'And I'll try and help Shona.'

The dodo and the rat held on to each other as Morag stretched out. With a snort of impatience, Shona kicked again and Morag tried to catch her foot. As the rowing boat steadied, Shona hooked the claws of her other foot over the rim and hauled the boat towards her, then threw herself on board with a crash. The back of the boat tipped out of the water and launched Bertie and Aldiss into the air. They smacked into Morag and landed with a bump on the bottom. Then with a horrible lurch, it tipped the other way, splashing all the occupants with icy water. Seconds later it righted itself leaving them breathless with shock.

'Sorry,' the dragon mumbled as she dragged her tail on board. A bedraggled Bertie gave her a dirty look, and shook his feathers.

'Being drenched is the least of our problems,' he snapped. 'We still have to climb those.'

Menacingly high, dark and brooding, the cliffs were as sheer and as ragged as a frozen waterfall. Morag swallowed hard as she craned her neck to see the top. How they were going to climb them she did not know.

Shona's face was set in concentration as she picked up the oars and began to pull against the strong swell of the ocean, which tugged and battered against them. Morag looked back at the *Sea Kelpie* and saw Kyle still standing on deck. They had agreed that he would stay behind and bring the boat round the coast to Murst Castle in the evening. He would know when to come when Bertie called him on a little walkie-talkie he had given him. Kyle waved when he saw Morag and she waved back. He must have seen how scared she looked because he smiled and gave her the thumbs up, as if to tell her not to worry.

'Do you really think we'll be able to climb all the way up there,' the rat asked her nervously.

Morag tried to smile. 'Of course we can. It'll be a piece of cake,' she said, sounding as confident as she could even though she was feeling quite the opposite.

'I'd rather be *eating* a piece of cake,' the rat replied wistfully. He tugged his hat down in a vain attempt to ward off the spray that drenched them. 'Or a piece of cheese...' he added to himself.

Bouncing over the high waves, they held on for dear life as Shona rowed them to the edge of the cliffs. They scoured the rock-face for a ledge to climb onto but none presented itself. Then Bertie spied a half hidden shelf a little way down. Shona wasted no time in rowing over. When close enough she set the oars down and let the swell carry the boat into the rock face with a bump that made them all jolt backwards.

'Bertie, can you go first?' Shona shouted at the terrified looking bird over the smashing of the waves.

The dodo looked at her uncertainly. Recognising his fear, Morag offered to go first instead, but the bird refused. 'If I can bring stone dragons back to life, I can climb this cliff,' he assured her. 'Right then!' He stood up. He adjusted his satchel across his back, flicked his tail, flapped his short wings a couple of times and crouched, ready to launch. A bemused Aldiss watched with interest. 'Here goes!'

The dodo reluctantly reached for the nearby rock shelf and caught it with his beak. Using both wings (and with a helpful shove from Shona) he scraped his round body on to the ledge, swung his claws behind him and hauled himself up. He lay there panting for a few seconds.

'Are you all right, Bertie?' Morag called.

He waved that he was, and the girl sighed with relief. She turned to Aldiss. He was too small to reach up to the plateau by himself, so Morag scooped him up and threw him there. He landed with a roll next to the exhausted Bertie, quickly got to his feet and scampered to the edge. Once he had given the girl the thumbs up, he clambered over to his feathered friend and helped him to sit up.

Morag went next. She stood up carefully with the boat tipping dangerously beneath her feet. Leaning over she grabbed a sharp crag with both hands and, using all of her strength, heaved herself out of the boat. A helpful shove on the bottom from Shona sent her scrambling over the ledge. Trembling with adrenalin and fear, and shaking with the cold, she sat down next to Bertie and Aldiss and gave them a weak smile.

For Shona, scaling the sheer, slippery rock-face was trickier. She grabbed a rope from the boat and slung it around her neck. The craft dipped and dived, throwing her off balance. Each time she reached out for the ledge the boat was whipped away by the swell. After a few false starts, she snatched a good hold on the rock. With a mighty heave she swung herself up and crawled over to her friends. She lay down on the wet stone and panted to catch her breath.

'What about the boat?' Aldiss asked as he watched it bash off the rocks.

'We'll have to leave it,' replied the dragon weakly. 'We've got more important things to think about.' She stared at the cliff looming above them and suddenly felt afraid. What had she been thinking about? There was no way they were going to climb this.

'Are you okay, Shona?' asked Morag, placing her hand on the dragon's shoulder.

'What? Er...yes, fine. Just plotting our route,' she said. She did not want to share her fears with anyone else, as they all looked nervous enough already. Shona rose to her feet, picked up the rope and quickly tied it around her waist. She handed an end to Morag and instructed her to do the same. Bertie and Aldiss followed until all four were roped together .

'This climb is going to be extremely difficult and dangerous,' Shona said firmly. 'We'll take it nice and slow and if anyone wants to stop, just ask. We do this properly, okay? I don't want any silly business,' she added with a knowing look at Aldiss. The rat looked aghast at the implication. 'Just keep climbing, don't look down and before you know it we'll be at the top. Are you ready?'

The other three nodded. No-one said a word.

'Good, then we'll get going,' the dragon said, staring uneasily at the sheer cliff in front of her. Without looking down, she began to look for good footholds. Reaching high, her claws closed around some fissures in the stone and, gripping tightly, she heaved her body up, her back legs scrabbling for toeholds. Slowly the dragon began her ascent, all the time aware of the crashing of the waves and the rocks below her. Morag allowed the dragon to go a couple of metres before the rope between them tightened and she started to climb. As she levered herself up the sharp outcrops her boots slipped against the wet rock. She dropped and swung on the rope, scraping her thin body off the raw seam of stone.

'Are you all right, Morag?' Shona called from above, her tail swinging as she fought to keep her balance. 'Do you want to go down? If it's too difficult, I'll go on alone.'

'No, don't do that. I'm fine,' the girl cried. 'We must keep going.'

Aldiss looked to Bertie for guidance. The dodo's eyes said it all: despite his fear, Bertie was determined not to let Shona and Morag down so when it came to his turn to start climbing, he launched himself at the rock face. The rat was cheered by his friend's resolve, and threw himself into the climb.

At last all four were climbing. Up the relentless rock face they rose, slipping and sliding on the crags. They were soon scraped from falls caused by ill-placed fingers, claws and paws. Still, on they went, ignoring the smash of the spray on the rocks. When Morag looked down at Bertie and Aldiss she saw how high they now were above the incisor-sharp rocks. One mistake, one slip, and they would all plummet down on top of them.

At last, when every last ounce of strength seemed used, when each thought they could go on no more, they saw Shona grip the edge of the cliff face and haul herself up and over the plateau. She stood and pulled the rope taut until Morag scrambled up beside her. Together they drew up Bertie and Aldiss then fell exhausted to the ground. They stayed there for a few minutes, enjoying the soft damp grass beneath their bodies and the soothing, earthy scent of the land. They had made it. They were alive and had a chance of saving Montgomery.

After a while, Shona sat up and looked around. It had been years since she had been on this part of the island and it had changed dramatically. When she had been a dragonlet—an infant dragon—it had been a mass of ferns and bushes. Now there was a neat patchwork of fields containing what looked like root vegetables and wheat. Each was marked into squares by stone dykes. The friends found they were sitting at the side of a neat pathway running the length of a field of raspberry bushes, their fruit long plucked and their leaves battered by the elements. Just beyond the fields was a village of peat-roofed houses. A dirt track ran to a fork in the road. To their left the track led to the fields, to their right into a large, wild forest full of ancient trees. Shona was shocked to see how much the forest had grown in the thirty years since she had last been here. It was sprawling westwards, almost to the coast. Looming over it all, menacing and shrouded in the dank mist that often swallowed the island whole, was Ben Murst, the island's only mountain.

'Glad to be home again?' Morag asked her.

The dragon smiled wanly. 'It's not the home I remember. Not now all the dragons are gone,' she replied, then with a sigh added, 'Come on you lot, let's get going, we've got a long way to go. We need to take the forest path to the castle. It's a few hours walk and we have to get there before the night draws in again.'

'But it's only morning now!' Aldiss said before anyone else could.

'Yes, but night falls early in the forest,' Shona said mysteriously, 'and there's a lot of nasty creatures in there that would like to have us all for dinner.'

Aldiss squeaked in fright. 'I-Isn't there another way round?' he said, black eyes wide.

'We don't have any choice,' Morag said getting to her feet. 'Come on, let's go. We've got a friend who needs our help!'

'Stay clear of the village,' the dragon warned. 'We don't want anyone knowing we're here, you never know who is on Mephista's side. Surprise is the only advantage we have. So long as we can keep our presence here a secret...'

'Um, Shona,' Morag interrupted. She pointed at something behind the dragon. 'I think it's a little bit too late for that.'

Shona scowled. 'What do you mean? We've only just arrived. No-one should know we're here...'

She turned to see what the girl was pointing at. In the distance, carrying pitchforks and other crude weapons, villagers were streaming out of the houses and heading in their direction.

'What do we do?' squealed Aldiss, running around in circles and tying himself up in frantic knots of anxiety.

'We run from them!' said the dodo flapping his wings.

'We fight them!' the dragon growled.

'We talk to them!' said Morag.

'Talk to them?' cried the others in unison.

Shona snapped: 'Do you really think talking's going to stop them from capturing us and handing us over to the castle?'

'Yes, talking is the best way out of this,' replied

Morag. 'They are only doing this because they are frightened of *us*.'

'The girl talks sense,' Henry interjected from the folds of Morag's coat.

'Besides,' she continued, 'they might be able to help.'

As the crowd advanced, Morag began to doubt her sensible suggestion.

What if Shona, Bertie and Aldiss were right and this wasn't a good idea? What if the villagers were out to harm them? She swallowed hard. She could only trust her instinct and hope for the best as the large group of armed, angry villagers drew closer.

chapter ten

They were a motley crew of muddy-clothed farm-hands and women in aprons and headscarves. They advanced, brandishing their weapons.

'Are you sure about this Morag?' Bertie whispered nervously.

'I...er...think so,' she replied. 'Listen everyone, let *me* deal with them. Humans are not used to talking animals.'

Shona snorted. 'Well these humans will have to get used to it quickly! I've got a lot to say to them about them being here. This is a *dragon* homeland. They're the ones who shouldn't be here!'

'Please Shona, let me do the talking.'

'Fine!' the dragon said moodily and uttered not another word.

Morag waited until the crowd were nearly upon them before walking forward, her hand outstretched in friendship as she'd seen nice adults do. The nearest villager, a woman, jabbed a pitchfork at her.

'Who are you?' she demanded, her long wild hair billowing in the cold morning wind.

'Morag MacTavish,' replied the girl. 'Pleased to meet you...?'

'And what are *these?*' the woman snarled at the

dragon and the dodo standing behind Morag.

'These are my friends...' Morag began, but she got no further for the woman interrupted her.

'Friends? You've brought vermin to our island!' She glared at Aldiss who bristled visibly at this insult. 'Who are you? And what do you want on this side of the DarkIsle?' the woman demanded.

'If I could just explain...' tried Morag.

'Are you spies from the castle come to check we are working? Eh? Is that what you're here for? Are we all supposed to quake at that giant lizard?'

'No, no! We've come in peace,' replied Morag, feeling Shona snort a cloud of disgruntled smoke on the back of her head. 'You can see we have no weapons,' she added quickly as the woman took another step forward. Her pitchfork was now almost touching Morag's nose. 'We...we...' Morag's thoughts raced around her head furiously as she tried to come up with an excuse as to why they were there. 'We've been shipwrecked,' she lied. 'We were washed ashore on the rocks. Can you help us? We need food and dry clothing.'

The woman eyed the girl suspiciously. She turned to her fellow villagers to garner their thoughts, but they did not seem able to offer anything other than a few menacing grunts at the newcomers. She turned back and threatened Morag again with the pitchfork.

'I don't believe you,' she snarled.

There were shouts of 'Go get her, Esmeralda!' from the crowd, which only served to strengthen the woman's conviction that Morag and her friends were dangerous.

'I say we skin the lizard and kill the rat, roast the bird and sell the girl back to the castle! That'll teach you to come spying on us,' she shouted.

There was cheering and clapping all round.

'No! No! You've got us all wrong,' protested Morag, but her cries fell on deaf ears.

'Let them go, Esmeralda,' said a thin wavering voice that rose from the jeers and silenced the crowd.

Morag peered behind the woman with the pitchfork to see who had spoken. At first she saw no-one, but then people began to move out of the way to allow a little elderly woman wrapped in a woollen cloak to shuffle forward. She had short grey hair and wore broken glasses.

'This is no way to welcome visitors to Dragon's End,' she said, addressing Esmeralda.

'But, mother, they could be dangerous. Things are bad enough without us trusting complete strangers.' She scowled. 'After what happened, I would have thought you of all people would know that.'

'After what happened we need all the friends we can get,' the old lady snapped. The younger woman made to say something back, but thought better of it, for she folded her arms and kept her mouth closed tight. Her mother smiled at Morag, revealing a set of yellowing teeth. She held out her hand.

'Now, dear,' she said, 'you must remind me…is this what we do to welcome you to Murst? Shake hands? It's been so long, I almost can't remember.'

Unsure what else to do, Morag took the old lady's hand and shook it gently. The hand was warm, but the skin was leathery, as if the woman did a lot of hard work.

'Welcome to Murst,' she said. 'My name is Ivy. You've met my daughter Esmeralda, and these are our neighbours and friends. Now, who might you be and how did you get here?'

Morag hastily introduced herself and her friends, and repeated her story that they were victims of a shipwreck. Ivy listened carefully and then chuckled.

'What's so funny?' Morag asked.

'I know you haven't been shipwrecked. I know why you're here,' Ivy replied. She turned to the villagers and said loudly, 'Friends! The Ancient One has arrived! At last!' A huge cheer went up from the villagers and they waved their weapons in the air. 'Prepare some food to welcome our guests!' She turned back to Morag. 'You'll stay and eat.' It was an order not a request.

'*Ancient One?*' Morag whispered to the others as they followed Ivy up the path to the village. 'What does she mean?'

Aldiss looked at Bertie accusingly.

'She wasn't referring to me!' said the dodo petulantly.

Morag smiled at this but Shona looked worried.

'We shouldn't go with them,' she said, covering her mouth with a claw. 'If we hang around here, word will get back to the castle in no time.'

'But what can we do?' replied Morag, under her breath.

'Leave!' hissed Shona.

'Your friends will be free to do as they wish once you've eaten,' Ivy called back. 'But not before then.'

The dragon scowled.

***

The village of Dragon's End consisted of a mud track lined by identical stone houses with peat roofs. Single storied and small, they had no front garden; only a large stone step that led up to the front door. Smoke curled from the chimneys, rising white and ghost-like into the grey Murst morning. There was one shop, which looked like the houses except that it boasted a sign painted with bright red curling letters: 'Dragon's End Municipal Stores'. In the middle of the village, next to a stone well, was a squat roundhouse and it was here that Ivy led them.

'Come, Ancient One,' she said, pushing open the door. 'And friends. Please enter and make yourselves comfortable. The food will arrive shortly.'

Inside, the large circular room was softly lit

by a ring of small windows set just beneath the roof. It was empty save for a pile of earth-coloured cushions piled up in the middle. This, Ivy explained, was where the villagers held their council, where they passed laws, and where the court sat.

'We used to have parties here too,' she confessed, then added sadly, 'Although we've not had much to celebrate recently.'

As she wandered around, Morag noticed the intricate carvings on the posts that held up the roof. Someone with obvious skill had carved rabbits and deer and other animals into the wood. There were birds and berries and...Morag frowned... was that an aeroplane? A train? A rocket? How, when they were so cut off, did the Dragon's End villagers know about life in the human world? Ivy saw her looking.

'Ah,' she said taking a tray of bread and cheese from a young boy, 'you're admiring our posts. Adam carved those from memory. He got here two years ago, but some of us have been here much longer. He was quite a talented artist.' She sighed and looked pained.

'Was?' Bertie asked, accepting a hunk of bread from Ivy's tray.

Tears formed in the old woman's eyes. 'The big apes took him away. Anyone who is taken away is never seen again.'

'What happened?' Morag asked. Bertie pulled a cushion nearer as Aldiss curled up beside him.

Only Shona, who was a little way away, did not move.

'It was about a week ago,' Ivy explained. 'We have very little food because the people in the castle take nearly everything we grow, so the men went hunting in the forest,' Ivy continued. 'Within half an hour they came running back, chased by a group of strange creatures.'

'What did they look like?' asked Bertie.

'They were like gorillas. Silver-haired gorillas. Only they had four arms each,' she said, leaving Morag to exchange looks with Bertie and Aldiss. 'They were dressed like hunters and came right into the village. They took our strongest men.'

'Didn't you try to put up a fight?' Shona asked.

'Yes, but they were too strong for us. They quickly captured three of our men and we had to admit defeat. Adam was among them. They headed back towards the castle.'

'I'm so sorry,' said Morag, who knew what it was like to be imprisoned there. 'What do you think has happened to them?'

'They're probably slaves now,' Ivy admitted. 'You'd think they'd leave us alone. We produce all their food and need all our strong men because we have to do everything by hand...not like on the mainland.'

'You know about the mainland?' Morag gasped.

'Of course we do, dear,' Ivy replied. 'Where else do you think we come from? None of us are from Murst originally. Esmeralda and I are from

Glasgow, and the others are from all over the country.'

'And you'd never heard of the DarkIsle until you got here?' asked Shona.

'No. And if anyone had told me about it I wouldn't have believed them.'

'How did you get here?' said Morag.

'We were kidnapped from our homes and brought here as slaves. Most of us have been on Murst for thirty-odd years—although five more arrived recently—and most of the children were born here.'

'Haven't you ever tried to escape?' asked Morag.

'Of course we have, but Murst is not like other islands. It's very difficult to leave if you don't know how,' she sobbed. 'Besides, it's impossible to get hold of a boat here. We tried making one, but they found out and destroyed it *and* our village as a punishment. We spent the winter in tents until we could rebuild our homes. The people of Murst Castle are evil. All they care about is having slaves to do whatever they want, whenever they want.'

There was a silence as everyone chewed over what Ivy had just told them. Then Morag remembered what Ivy had said previously.

'When you found us you mentioned something about an Ancient One...'

'I saw it in the tea leaves,' the old woman explained. 'The Ancient One will return soon to save us all.'

'Tea leaves?' Aldiss squeaked. 'You've got tea here?'

'Tiny portions are included as part of our rations from the castle. It comes in by pirate ships.'

'But,' the rodent continued, 'how can tea leaves tell you anything?'

'I read them,' Ivy responded proudly. 'I'm a seer. I can look into the future and tell you what might happen. The tea leaves told me the Ancient One will free us from this horrible place forever.'

'And did the tea leaves describe this Ancient One?' asked Bertie, fanning his tail feathers in expectation. 'Did they mention his wonderful plumage or impressive beak?'

'No,' said Ivy. Bertie scowled. 'First of all I saw that the Ancient One would have a strong heart and a kind manner...'

Bertie and Aldiss immediately looked at Morag.

'And then I saw the Ancient One's long tail...'

'I knew it!' squealed Aldiss, jumping to his feet and whipping his tail from side to side. 'It's me isn't it?'

'I'm afraid not,' said Ivy. Aldiss dropped his tail to the floor with a disappointed thud. 'And she would be green...'

'It's Shona...' whispered Morag. 'You're the Ancient One.'

Shona, sitting nearby, snorted sceptically, sending up little bellows of dark smoke. 'Tea leaves!' she scolded. 'No one can predict the future, no matter what the method. It's all a load of Swamp Sprouts.'

Morag decided it would be best to change the subject. 'We'd like to thank you for your hospitality,' she began.

'You're welcome,' Ivy replied. She moved towards the doorway.

'It's been wonderful to meet you and the other villagers,' Morag continued.

'Likewise.'

'But,' the girl said, getting to her feet, 'we must leave now. We need to get to the castle. You were right about us not being shipwrecked. We came here to get our friend back. He's a prisoner and we must get to him before something terrible happens.'

Ivy smiled. 'But I can't let you go, my dear,' she said, her hand gripping the door handle. 'Your dragon *has* to save us. And I can't let you go off into the woods by yourselves. You might be killed by the wolves or the other creatures that live there.' She gave an involuntary shudder. 'No, I think it is best that you all stay here until we decide what the Ancient One has to do next.'

Before the last word left her lips, Shona, as quick as lightening, got to her feet and growled at her. 'You will not tell us what to do!' she snarled, making angry puffs of smoke pour from her nostrils. 'We're leaving and that's that.'

Morag quickly placed a hand on Shona's shoulder in a vain attempt to calm her.

'What the Ancient One means,' she told the terrified Ivy, 'is that she's probably *destined* to go to the castle. After all, she's no good to you here, doing nothing, is she?'

'Um…no, I suppose not,' the woman whispered.

'And perhaps you are meant to help us get there?' Morag continued, pleased with her train of thought.

'I-I suppose we could do something for you,' Ivy said slowly. 'Stay here a minute while I consult the other elders.'

She shuffled out of the door and locked it behind her. Shona gave a low grumble in the back of her throat, snatched the handle and angrily yanked the door off its hinges. She threw it into the middle of the room, narrowly missing Aldiss and Bertie, who ducked just in time.

'Shona!' Morag scolded. 'Calm down!'

'Calm down? She thinks she can lock us up. Well, she can't. This is *my* island. Mine, not theirs!' the dragon snapped.

'They're prisoners here too,' a complacent tinny voice said. Henry had been watching everything with interest. 'It's not their fault that they're here, Madam Dragon. Just as the loss of your dear family was not yours.'

'Hmmph,' Shona snorted, and stomped to the other side of the room, where she turned her back on her friends and sat in a smoky huff.

Aldiss went to pacify her, but was stopped by Morag. 'Leave her for a few minutes,' she said. 'She's sad more than angry.'

Just then Ivy appeared in the doorway. The astonished old woman stared at the broken door-frame. Her mouth hung open in a perfect oval.

'Shona felt trapped,' Aldiss explained.

'She...er...has a thing about cages,' added Bertie.

'I'm sorry about your door, but you needn't have locked it,' Morag said.

Ivy said nothing. She stepped over the bits of broken wood and approached Morag. 'Are you and the Ancient One really here to free us?' Ivy asked quietly, hope brimming in her eyes.

Morag was taken aback. Her only intention was to get Montgomery back. She gave Ivy a weak smile. 'Well, to be honest, that's not why we came here...' she said. 'But if we can do anything to help, we will.'

'Then we'll help you,' the old woman said. 'We have someone who will guide you through the forest then get you inside the castle.'

'Oh thank you,' Morag replied gratefully. 'And now, we really must leave.'

'I understand. I've instructed her to take you this instant,' Ivy replied. 'Time is also running out for our friends.'

chapter eleven

Outside the roundhouse, they found a hooded figure waiting next to an old horse and cart.

'Now,' said Ivy, handing Morag a bundle wrapped in a sand-coloured cloth. 'Take this. You'll need provisions for the road—bread and cheese and some cake.'

'Oh, I don't think we'll need this. We have Bertie's magic bag to give us food,' Morag protested trying to give the bundle back.

'Magic?' laughed the old woman. 'What good will magic do you in that wood? It doesn't work. Even the great Devlish himself couldn't use magic in *there*. It's the trees, you see, they suck magic right out of the air. No, not even magic can help you in there, so you best take this.'

Morag accepted the food parcel gratefully and thanked the old woman. Bertie gazed at her, worried. Before he could say anything, the girl reassured him.

'We'll be fine,' she said firmly, although she didn't believe it herself. 'Come on, let's go. We've got a long journey ahead of us.'

The old woman took them to the cart. 'Let me introduce your guide,' she said. 'This is my granddaughter...'

The figure, black cloak billowing in the wind, turned round and pushed down her hood. Morag gasped. 'Chelsea!' she said, recognising Mephista's maid at once.

'The one and only,' the girl replied with a laugh. 'I see you've still got that big gold medallion on you.'

Morag's hand flew protectively to Henry.

'Still not wanting to give it up?' Chelsea smiled, but there was no warmth in her eyes. 'I'll give you a good price for it.'

'He doesn't belong to me. He's his own person.'

'Well said,' Henry piped up.

Chelsea looked surprised. 'It talks as well?' She gawped at him. 'Are you sure you don't want to sell it?'

There was something unpleasant about her attitude that made Morag recoil.

'Hey! There'll be none of that kind of talk here,' snapped Ivy, giving Chelsea a clip around the back of the head. 'You leave that girl's necklace alone. You've got plenty without coveting everyone else's things.'

'Ow, that hurt!' Chelsea protested.

'Now get on with what you've been asked to do,' the old woman ordered. 'And I'll hear none of your protests neither.'

Chelsea opened her mouth to answer back but thought better of it. She climbed into the driver's seat, took up the reins and sat sullenly while Morag, Bertie and Aldiss climbed aboard. Shona realised she was too big for the cart and would have to walk alongside.

'Goodbye,' Ivy called, waving as they trundled towards the Deep Dark Wood. 'Be careful! And watch out for the wolves. Good luck!'

'Did she say 'wolves'?' asked Aldiss as the cart trundled between the trees. He shivered.

'Don't worry,' Morag replied, 'we've got Shona to protect us.'

She smiled at her friend. The dragon grimaced; she was still in too much of a bad mood to share Morag's optimism. Aldiss wasn't convinced either, but he felt better for having the dragon with them. He chose a comfortable spot in some hay that had been left on the floor, curled up and soon was fast asleep. Morag, with Henry still around her neck, nestled down beside an anxious Bertie, who was almost hanging off the edge of the cart trying to peer between the trees.

'You know,' he said, 'I've never seen so many different species of trees in one place—and so tightly packed together.'

'Maybe one day you can come back and study them properly,' said Morag.

'I wouldn't do that if I were you,' Chelsea said from the front of the cart. 'Those trees are liable to eat you if you get close enough.'

'Don't be so silly. Trees don't eat birds,' Bertie said imperiously, gesturing to the passing branches that loomed low over the cart. 'Trees are our friends. They allow us to build nests in them, they provide shelter and...'

But the look Chelsea gave him made it clear she was *not* being silly. 'Not these trees. They'd grab you right out of this cart! Don't forget: they're Murst trees. Nothing here is what it seems,' she said.

Bertie gulped and glanced around at the forest with a new sense of fear.

'So Morag, my gran was too busy talking about that dragon to tell me what you're doing back here,' Chelsea continued. 'I thought you wouldn't show your face after what happened last time.' The girl turned and gave Morag a sly look.

'We need to get into the castle,' was all Morag would say. 'Can you get us in?'

'Dunno,' replied Chelsea. 'What's it worth?' She nodded down at Henry. Morag swiftly tucked him out of sight.

'Our eternal gratitude?' she replied tartly.

'Hmmph,' Chelsea snorted. 'I don't want your gratitude. What use it that to anybody? I want something more valuable than that.'

'How about your freedom?' Bertie asked.

Chelsea turned right round in her seat to face him.

'My freedom? How can you give me that?'

'Once we've got what we've come for, we're leaving by boat,' replied Morag. 'You can come with us.'

'You're not just saying that?'

'No! I promise.'

That seemed to satisfy Chelsea, and she turned back to concentrate on driving the cart.

Morag frowned at Bertie as if to say: *that girl might be trouble.* He nodded knowingly. With a wing, feathers splayed, he pointed to Chelsea then to one of his eyes and Morag understood what he was trying to say: We need to keep an eye on her. Morag nodded.

'You lot are awfully quiet back there,' Chelsea said. 'I hope you're not changing your minds.'

'We're...uh...just keeping an eye out for these trees,' Morag said, gazing around her in case the girl decided to look round again.

'Good idea,' smiled their driver. 'Look out for the hungry ones!'

To Chelsea, who knew this area well, Murst's wild woods looked even darker and more menacing than usual. Apart from the thin shafts of light that cut through the heavy canopy of winter-bare branches, the forest was filled with twisted shadows. Ancient elms, oaks and pines towered above them, creaking and sighing in the wind as the cart trundled along the path towards the castle.

As they moved deeper into the forest Morag joined Aldiss and Bertie to huddle together in the hay, becoming increasingly aware of the strange rustlings and animal calls that seemed to come from all directions.

'W-what was that?' said Aldiss, starting with fright.

'It was probably only Shona stepping on a twig,' said Morag as the dragon caught up with them.

'There it is again!' he said, his tail starting to quiver.

'Don't panic,' replied Morag, stroking his fur. 'Sit closer to me and Bertie. We're not afraid—are we Bertie?'

'Morag!' Bertie hissed. 'I think we're being followed.'

'Are you sure you're not imagining things?'

'No, I'm not,' he said urgently. 'We're definitely being followed. I've been seeing the same sets of eyes for the last half hour.'

'He's right,' said Shona. 'The smell of the forest has changed.'

Now *that* got Morag's attention. Her eyes opened wide and she sat up.

'What do you mean?' she asked nervously.

'Look,' the dodo replied. He pointed to a clump of bushes. 'Over there, and there. And back there too.'

Morag followed Bertie's outstretched wing and thought she could make out large dark shapes shifting behind the spiky greenery of the undergrowth. Wherever she looked, huge yellow eyes glinted hungrily in the shadows, and then vanished back into the dark. She thought she heard a low snarl from somewhere nearby. She gulped and turned to Chelsea. 'I think you should try and make the horse go faster. We're being followed.'

'Oh don't worry about that, it'll just be the wolves,' the girl replied. 'They don't tend to attack during the day. We'll be fine.'

This did not make Morag feel any better. The horse whinnied nervously, its ears flicking, listening for danger.

'I really think we should move faster...' Morag tried again.

'Look, are you driving this cart or am I?' Chelsea snapped, her voice ringing out through the forest. A million rustling creatures took fright and rushed from the path. Birds flew into the air, rodents burrowed deeper, but the shadows around them seemed to move closer.

'Just the wolves she says!' Bertie repeated incredulously.

'WOLVES! Where?' Aldiss shrieked, glancing around him.

'Shhhhhhhh!'

'Sorry,' mumbled the rat, eyes wide as something went *SNAP!* in the forest beyond the path.

'What was that? What was that?' he yelped, leaping into Morag's arms.

'It's nothing,' she said, although she could not be sure. The trees seemed to be crowding closer, the bushes thicker, and the shadows darker. And although she had not actually seen a wolf yet, she was sure she had caught something out the corner of her eye: something large prowling through the undergrowth. But when she looked there was nothing there.

'Y-you're probably right, Morag,' stammered Bertie. 'There's nothing to...AAAWWK!

He jumped in an explosion of feathers as an enormous wolf pounced from the bushes and bounded after them. It was long and lean and the biggest animal Morag had ever seen. Its mean eyes never left hers as it bared its razor sharp teeth. Morag caught her breath, and shrieked, 'Chelsea! Faster!'

Chelsea saw the wolf and whipped the reins. 'Hold on in the back!' she yelled. Her horse, wide-eyed and sweating, screamed as it flew into a gallop, dragging the cart bumping behind. Shona dived into the shrubs out of the way as the huge grey wolf tore past her. The dragon quickly regained her senses as seven more wolves stole out from the bushes and joined the chase. Chelsea, clinging to the side of the cart, her arms straining to keep hold of the reins, screamed at Morag. 'Look under...get them...!'

The wolves were baying and barking and snapping. The horse, running for its life, squealed and Aldiss was in her arms, whimpering in fright.

'What? I can't hear you!' Morag shouted. She was nearly thrown out of the cart as it swerved and threatened to overturn.

'Under the hay! I put them there!' Chelsea screamed back. '*The swords! Use the swords!*'

Morag dropped Aldiss with a bump. 'Help me look, they're here somewhere!' she instructed him and Bertie as the cart swayed and jolted with the wolves snapping at the wheels. The three friends began to scrabble at the hay, throwing it up and over the side. Some of it landed on the face of the lead wolf, who snarled it away. Morag pulled up the hay in handfuls, as her friends rooted for the weapons.

'What's this?' Aldiss squeaked, tugging something with his teeth. Morag helped him lift a long heavy object that was covered in a sack cloth. She threw it off and uncovered two swords with long gleaming blades. Grabbing one and swaying dangerously from side to side, Morag got to her feet and tried to hold it steady.

'Come and get it!' she cried as the lead wolf growled at her, saliva dripping from its lips.

No sooner had the words left her mouth, than the cart smashed into a knotted tree root in the road. Morag was thrown into the air and crashed into Bertie and Aldiss on the floor of the cart. They heard the sound of splintering wood as the wheels buckled beneath them. The cart tilted and Aldiss was swept off, clawing and squeaking, towards the wolf's ravenous jaws. Bertie dived forward, caught Aldiss's tail in his beak and yanked him back just as the wolf's fangs snapped together in mid-air.

With a terrible crack the shaft gave way, crashing the cart and releasing the terrified horse. It reared up out of its restraints and galloped off into the forest.

The wolves surrounded the cart as Morag helped

Bertie and Aldiss to their feet and checked that Chelsea was all right. Clasping the sword tightly, Morag looked unblinkingly into the wicked eyes of the lead wolf. She could have sworn it was actually grinning at her. With her heart beating furiously, she brandished the sword and dared it to attack. The wolf licked its lips as it sized her up. As Bertie and Aldiss looked on, terrified, Morag stood still and held her sword steady. She knew that if they ran, they would be hunted down and torn to pieces. They had a better chance of survival if they stayed and fought.

The wolf edged a few steps closer, its fur raised and its lips curled back in a bloodthirsty growl. Snarling and snapping it readied itself to launch at the girl.

'Oh no you don't!' a voice called.

The wolf jumped when a large, green scaly body bounded into the clearing.

'Shona!' cried Morag.

The wolf growled and bared his large teeth.

'Is that the best you can do?' Shona snorted. 'Now, I will give you one chance to leave my friends alone.'

The wolf turned from Morag and began to circle the dragon. It paused, threw its head back and howled. Its hunting call was enough to bring the others and before Morag knew what was happening Shona was surrounded. The dragon held her ground as the wolves gathered round her.

'Leave now or you'll be sorry!' she warned.

The lead wolf crouched to pounce, muscles quivering.

'Aaaaarrrrrrrrrrrrr!' the dragon roared as she unleashed a torrent of flames and smoke.

For a moment the air turned white with fiery heat. Then the smoke cleared, leaving a ring of stunned wolves with blackened, hairless muzzles. The leader blinked, sneezed, and scurried yelping into the forest, its tail between its legs. The rest of the pack followed, burned and smoking.

'Well,' said Shona to her astonished friends, '*they* won't be bothering us again.'

'You got here just in time,' beamed Bertie.

'I was nearly eaten!' cried Aldiss.

'Are *you* okay?' Shona asked Morag. The girl nodded and put down her sword. 'Thank you,' she said. 'Another moment and they would have had us for dinner.'

'I thought it would be best if I held back for a moment,' Shona explained. 'So I could take them by surprise when their attention was focused on you.'

'Now what?' asked Henry from around Morag's neck. 'The horse is gone and the cart is destroyed.'

'Now we walk,' replied Morag determinedly as she jumped to the ground. 'I'm not going to let a bunch of wolves stop us.'

She set off in the direction of the castle but stopped when she realised the others weren't following. 'Are you coming?'

'It's such a long way,' began Aldiss, still quivering.

'And we're only little,' added Bertie, looking at Shona hopefully. 'I don't think we can walk that far, especially Aldiss who is the littlest of us all.'

The dragon rolled her big yellow eyes and sighed. 'Get on,' she said, crouching to allow the animals to clamber on to her back. 'Morag? Chelsea? Do you need a lift too?'

Chelsea, who was quiet and shaking after their scare, was about to say 'yes', but was interrupted by Morag who was determined to get there under her own steam. 'No, we're fine. We'll walk,' she said. 'Are you coming, Chelsea?'

Annoyed that she was going to have to walk, Chelsea sullenly joined Morag and together the girls led the little band of friends through the forest.

***

The walk was long and hard, and wasn't made easier by the worsening weather. It grew colder and a sea wind started to howl through the trees, causing Aldiss to squeak with fright.

Morag pulled her hood up and tucked Henry under her collar to keep him warm. She stuck a frozen hand in her pocket and felt the reassuring shape of her missing parents' book. The familiar pang of sadness swept over her and she wondered where they were and if they were thinking about her. A flurry of snowflakes broke through the trees' canopy and landed on the sleeves of her coat. Normally snow would have delighted her, but this time she felt exposed, without warmth or comfort, and knew a heavy snowfall could be dangerous for them all, especially the cold-blooded Shona.

'How much further?' the dragon panted. She was shivering and had fallen behind.

'Not far,' Chelsea assured her. 'We'll be there soon enough.'

'Look! Over there!' Morag cried. 'The castle!'

Through the trees they saw the tall turrets in the distance, their flags guttering in the wind. The castle was still far off and it was another hour before they saw it again between the firs. It still looked formidable. The fortress of grey stone was pocked by narrow windows that glittered in the dimming light. Red banners hung from the ramparts were whipped by the vicious sea winds. High above, giant guards marched back and forth on unending patrols, carrying sharp pikes across their shoulders, their eyes vigilant for attack. Huge wooden gates held the castle's occupants inside and kept intruders out. These too were guarded by four giants standing to attention.

'There's no way we'll get past them,' Morag confided to Henry.

'Don't worry,' he told her. 'There *will* be a way.'

'What are you whispering about?' Chelsea asked.

'I was just wondering how you are going to get us into the castle,' Morag replied. She studied Chelsea to see how she would react. She was not sure the girl would keep her promise.

'Oh that's easy,' Cheslea replied. 'There's a door at the side that not many folk know about. It was supposed to be an escape route if the castle was ever attacked. It never has been, so no-one's ever used it and it's been forgotten about. Except by me. I'll go through the main gates and open it for you. You should get in without being seen.'

Chelsea's plan seemed too simple for Morag's liking, but it was their only hope, so she agreed to it.

'And you'll stick to your part of the bargain?' Chelsea asked, searching Morag's face for any signs of duplicity. 'You'll take me with you when you leave?'

'Yes. I promised didn't I?'

Before Chelsea could reply they were interrupted by a howl washing over the forest. Chelsea turned a deathly white. The sound continued, growing deeper, stronger, closer.

BWWWAAAAAAAARRRR!

'What's that?' Morag asked.

'The-the-Girallons. They-they're out hunting!' Chelsea squealed. 'That's their horn. We must hide! They'll kill us if they catch us!'

BWWWAAARRR! BWWWAAAAARRR! The horn sounded over and over, its tone flat and baleful. It rumbled through the forest like an elephant on the rampage.

'Quickly,' Morag urged. 'Hide in the bushes!'

Aldiss disappeared with a leap, and Bertie scurried under a shrub, but Shona was having some difficulty. She was quite large for a pigmy dragon, and it took her some frantic moments to find a bush large enough. Morag ran to the other side of the track and threw herself behind a fallen tree. She glanced up and saw Chelsea still standing in the pathway, frozen with fear.

'Chelsea! They'll see you!' Morag called, but the girl seemed not to hear. Morag scrambled to her feet and raced to her side. She seized Chelsea's arm and yanked her off the path. Although Chelsea was trembling, she did not resist and followed Morag to the hollow tree trunk. She crawled in first and Morag followed, just managing to hide herself as a group of hunters burst through the trees. She could hear the heavy pounding of their feet as they approached. A gruff voice barked an order and the hunters stopped just feet from them. Pressed against each other, Chelsea was curled up with her eyes shut tight.

Morag held her breath and willed the creatures to leave.

Sniff, sniff, sniff.

Someone—or some*thing*—sniffed the air immediately above them. It was all Morag could do to stop herself from crying out in fright.

Sniff, sniff, snuffle.

It got closer. *Sniff...*

Morag desperately tried not to make a sound. Her blood surged through her body, creating a great rushing in her ears that she was sure this hunter could hear.

Sniff. Grunt.

It was searching for something. Had it picked up her scent? She began to shake. She heard other feet walking, someone else talking, and the distraction caused whatever was sniffing to pause and growl at his companions. The sounds of movement stopped. The forest stopped. There was only silence.

The creature inhaled deeply and let out a satisfied snort, which confirmed Morag's greatest fear: it knew they were there. She closed her eyes as the thing climbed on to the dead tree, making it shudder. Four large grey hands gripped the edge of the hole just above her head as the creature leaned over to look inside. The rotten wood creaked and split and threatened to give way.

This is it, Morag thought. *We've been discovered.*

chapter twelve

'Tallow!' someone shouted as the creature pulled in closer. Bark crumbled in its hand. 'Tallow!' said the other voice again. 'Come on, we should be getting back to the castle. We're expected.'

'But they're here somewhere, I can smell them,' Tallow replied, his voice deep and hoarse. 'Just give me a few more minutes to prise them out.'

'You always think you can smell humans, Tallow,' another creature said. 'You are obsessed.'

'Obsessed with hunting them,' the one called Tallow replied with a sneer.

In her hiding place, Morag bit her lip in an effort not to scream.

'Brave hunters return!' a gruff voice screeched from the direction of the castle. 'Brave hunters return!'

'I'm busy right now,' Tallow barked in response, sullenly like a scolded child.

One of the Girallons roared loudly, the sound resonating violently through the forest. 'Tallow, leave it, we need to get back. You heard him. Come on,' one of the voices urged, sounding afraid.

'I can *get* it,' Tallow replied, stuffing two hands into the hollow tree and grabbing. Morag had to stop herself from gasping as one hand narrowly missed her face. 'Just give me a moment.'

'*Now*, Tallow!' his companion growled. 'He's calling us from the castle.'

Sure enough, the call came again, this time angry and threatening. There was an irritated sigh from Tallow and a shuffling sound as he shifted his weight. The tree rocked as he pulled himself upright and leapt back onto the path.

'You can hunt humans another day,' his fellow creature assured him, giving him a slap on the back. 'For now, we must obey Kang and return to the castle.'

As they stomped away, Morag peeked out, keen to see what these things looked like. She saw three huge creatures loping off, like large gorillas except that they had grey fur and four muscular arms. They wore blue and silver tunics, and around their waists were thick leather belts hung with weapons. All three carried bows and arrows.

Morag shuddered as they disappeared into the gloom of the forest. She ducked back inside the log, where Chelsea was still curled up with her eyes closed tightly.

'It's safe,' Morag reassured her, 'they're gone. You can come out now.'

As Morag stumbled back to the path, the others emerged from the undergrowth too, their faces tense with fear. Shona, Bertie and Aldiss hurried to Morag's side to make sure she had not been hurt. Shona hugged her tightly, crushing Morag against her great dragon chest. Morag could hear Shona's heart hammering.

'Thank goodness you're all right!' Shona cried.

'We thought you were done for,' squeaked Aldiss.

'So did I for a moment,' Morag replied, relief washing over her. 'But at least I got a look at those things.'

'I've never seen a real live Girallon before,' said Bertie. 'Only read about them in books. They're especially vicious.'

'We can't wait for them to come back,' said Chelsea. 'We have to get going. We need to get into that castle before anything else happens.'

***

Chelsea left them hiding in the dark undergrowth near the edge of the forest. From behind a screen of ferns, they watched her walk up to the castle gates where she spoke to the guards. Whatever she said seemed to satisfy them for they immediately stood to attention and let her pass. Then, without a backward glance, Chelsea slipped between the gates and was lost from sight.

They could do nothing more now but wait.

In her cramped position on the ground Morag was unbearably cold. She could no longer feel her feet, and her hands were aching from exposure to the wintery air. The wind had got up and was tugging at her coat with greedy fingers, threatening to pierce the thick red fabric and expose her to the elements. Trembling, she lifted her frozen hands to her mouth and blew on them. The heat gave her momentary relief, but she knew that within seconds her fingers would be numb once more. *Hurry up Chelsea*, she thought. She stared at the little side door half hidden in the failing light and willed it to open.

As the sun set and the afternoon drew its last gasp of the winter light, the forest grew dark and full of mysterious noises. Aldiss could not prevent himself from letting out a whimper. Morag picked him up and gave him a cuddle and together they watched for Chelsea. The narrow doorway looked about a head taller than Morag. She was confident she could get inside with Aldiss and Bertie, but worried about Shona.

'I should've realised it'd be too small for a dragon,' Morag whispered.

'I'll get in there with no bother,' the dragon assured them. 'I'm quite flexible you know.'

'Now's your chance to prove it,' Bertie snorted. 'The door is opening.'

There was Chelsea peering out. She was holding up a storm lantern which cast dark shadows across her face.

'Aldiss and I will go first,' Bertie said, taking charge. 'Morag and Shona, you should wait until we're inside and then follow.'

They nodded.

'Are you ready Aldiss?'

The little rat saluted smartly and squeaked that he was.

'See you inside,' Bertie told them before they could protest.

The dodo and the rat emerged cautiously from the shadows, searching for any signs of danger. Aldiss twitched his whiskers, Bertie fluffed his feathers, and both took a deep breath. A furtive check up at the castle ramparts confirmed the guards had not seen them. They scuttled across the wasteland between the woods and the castle. Aldiss, brown and camouflaged against the muddy ground, vanished almost at once. Morag did not see him again until his tiny black silhouette appeared in the doorway. Bertie's dull plumage also kept him hidden, except for one thing: his white tail bobbed like a beacon across the grass. Before long, he too was safe inside. Morag sighed with relief. 'Our turn,' she said to the medallion inside her coat.

'Head down and as fast as you can,' he replied. 'The guards won't be gone for long.'

Morag stuck her hand inside her coat pocket and felt for her book. It was still there. After a quick nod to Shona, Morag scrambled from the undergrowth and ran across the scrubland. Within seconds, she was through the door and hugging Bertie and Aldiss.

'Where's Shona?' Aldiss inquired.

'She's right behind me.'

Shona staggered up to the doorway and stuck her head inside. The dragon looked relieved that she had managed to cross the open area without being seen, but that look was soon wiped from her face as she realised she was never going to squeeze through the narrow doorframe.

'If I...er...just turn this way...and...um...' she huffed, releasing little puffs of smoke from her nostrils as she became agitated. 'Just give me a... minute,' she insisted, wriggling and twisting and squeezing.

Morag stopped her. 'I think it would be best if you waited outside for us. You're too big, you'll never get through, and we can't risk you getting stuck. We won't be long. Give us a couple of hours. If we're not out by then, go and get help.'

'I'm sorry Morag, I really wanted to help,' Shona said sorrowfully.

'You'll be helping us by staying hidden outside,' the girl replied, giving her a hug. 'We'll see you soon. Now go and hide before someone sees you.'

With one last doleful look at her friends, Shona pulled herself out of the doorway and disappeared into the dark. Morag turned to the others.

'Let's go.'

As she said this, Chelsea's lantern was blown out by the draft, plunging them into complete darkness. Despite her best efforts with matches, she could not get it going again.

'Never mind,' said Morag, sounding braver than

she was feeling. 'We'll just have to feel our way along this corridor.'

They stumbled along the rocky floor of the un-lit passage, unable to see where they were go-ing. A sudden blaze of light made Morag start. A spotlight appeared on the wall. She glanced around and saw Bertie strapping on a miner's helmet. His little black eyes twinkled and she could have sworn that he winked at her.

'Where did you get...?' she began and then remembered his satchel from which he could produce almost anything. 'Oh never mind,' she added. She barely reacted when a few moments later she found Aldiss wearing one too. The rat scampered on ahead, leading the way up the dark, dank corridor.

The passage seemed to have been cut from solid rock, for in every direction Aldiss and Ber-tie shone their torches they briefly highlighted identical stretches of roughly hewn stones, ceil-ing and floor. Morag thought it was as if some-one had carved a warren of passageways into the very core of the island. As they continued she realised that the floor was steadily climbing.

'Is it much further?' Morag asked Chelsea, who was walking up behind her.

'No. Here, let me pass will you? I'll go in front to check no-one's there when we get into the main part of the castle.'

She squeezed past Morag and walked ahead of the dodo and the rat. Through the beams of Aldiss and Bertie's lamps, they watched her shadowy figure reach a set of stone steps that led to a wooden door.

'Turn off your lights,' she whispered. 'If anyone is on the other side they'll see them straight away.'

They did and Bertie returned them to his satchel. Everyone's eyes had to adjust back to the darkness before Chelsea opened the door a crack and looked outside. They all held their breath.

Morag waited, her heart thumping and her mouth dry. Getting this far had seemed too easy and she was getting more worried that they could be caught at any moment. The corridor was dark and narrow, which was perfect for hiding, but if the inhabitants knew they were there, it was also the perfect trap. She watched as Chelsea slipped out. A dull light filtered into the corridor and they waited for a signal.

Moments went by and the friends whispered their worries to each other. What was taking Chelsea so long? Had she been caught? Morag was just about to sneak up to the doorway when the girl's face reappeared.

'It's all right,' she said in a loud whisper, 'the coast is clear.'

One by one they filed into the castle corridor. Morag immediately recognized it as the one that ran alongside the Great Hall. The floor was paved with broad flagstones; the walls were lined with silks and hung with tapestries; every door leading off the corridor was inlaid with intricate carvings; fine candelabras and sconces hung from the ceiling. The whole corridor, illuminated by candles and oil torches, glowed and flickered as they passed down it.

'I think Montgomery is being held in the dungeon,' Chelsea whispered, leading them to a doorway. 'It's down there.'

After a quick glance around, Morag pushed open the door and slipped inside, followed by Aldiss, Bertie and Chelsea.

As they went, nobody noticed the creature hiding in the shadows. As they sneaked down the stairwell into the dungeon below, nobody guessed he was following them. A skilful hunter, the creature steadily pursued his prey as they tip-toed down the winding stairs into the bowels of the castle.

The spiral stairwell was lit by flickering torches stuck at intervals in the wall high above their heads. There was a strong smell of burning and something else, something fishy and rotten. Morag put it down to the fact they were so near to the sea and that the tide was probably out, drying the seaweed on the beach. She dismissed it and continued to follow Chelsea.

'Is it much further?' Aldiss whined as he scuttled down the stairs after the girls. 'I don't like it down here.' The stone stairs were getting damper the further they went and he was afraid they would eventually run into water. He didn't like getting any bit of him wet, especially his paws.

'Oh stop whining, rat,' Henry said crossly. 'Living in Marnoch Mor has made you soft. Rats are supposed to like damp places like this. It's almost compulsory.'

'Eep!' squeaked Aldiss, ears twitching in the dim light. 'What was that?'

'What was what?' whispered Morag.

'I thought I heard something just now, something behind us.'

The creature froze.

'It's probably one of your cousins,' the medallion snapped.

In the shadows, the stalking creature shifted. Aldiss's ears flickered, searching for the direction of the sound. 'There it is again,' Aldiss whispered, his whiskers bristling.

'It was an echo,' said Chelsea.

Aldiss peered up into the gloom behind Bertie. 'No, I'm sure I heard something then, like a...like a...laugh.'

'You're imagining things,' Bertie said softly. He spread a wing around his friend's furry shoulders and gently turned him back round. 'Come on, there's nothing to worry about.'

But Aldiss wasn't convinced and kept looking back nervously. He was sure he had seen something out of the corner of his eye, but when he looked more closely whatever it was had gone. He shivered and kept pace with his friends.

At last, the stairs petered out and they found

themselves standing in a small corridor.

'Here we are,' Chelsea smiled at Morag, and motioned towards a heavy door. 'The dungeon is that way.'

Morag eyed her guide suspiciously. 'You go first,' she said, stepping back to allow Chelsea to pass. The maidservant smirked and went to step forward when there was a gust of wind from the stairwell. Both girls turned to look. A strong draught whirled down the stairs, extinguishing the torches. As they watched the winds started to gather, spinning at the bottom of the stairs. Soon it was a tornado, raging above their heads like an angry god. Morag watched with her mouth hanging open. Something deep inside snapped her into action. She came to her senses, yanked open the dungeon door and pushed her friends inside. As she was about to slip through, the tornado swept forward. Ice cold fingers of air reached out to her, grabbed her by the waist and lifted her off the floor. She was sucked towards the maelstrom.

'Heeeeelp!' she cried, reaching out for her horrified friends.

Aldiss managed to grab hold of Henry, who was dangling from Morag's neck. He held on for all he was worth, anchoring himself to the doorframe with one paw and pulling with the other, but the wind was strengthening. Bertie grabbed a hold of the rat, Chelsea held the bird and a tug of war ensued between the chain of friends and the wind above. It lasted for a few seconds before there was a sudden roar from the whirlwind and a long blowpipe emerged from its core.

Puff! A dart flew from its barrel and glanced off the rat's ear, ripping off the tip. Aldiss shrieked, and let go of Henry, falling to the floor. He looked up to see the medallion spinning off Morag's neck as she was sucked upwards into the blustering winds.

With a *Pop!* the tornado disappeared into thin air, taking the screaming girl with it. Aldiss scrambled to his feet, his head dull and unfocused. He frowned as he tried to work out what Bertie was shouting at him. He felt so sleepy. He stumbled and fell onto one knee. He tried to get up but slipped on the stone floor and collapsed. With a small sigh, he lay down and closed his eyes. Bertie and Chelsea immediately ran to his side.

'Aldiss! Aldiss!' the bird cried, but the rat did not respond. Bertie saw the arrow lying on the floor nearby and looked up at Chelsea. 'He was hit,' he said as he cradled his friend in his wing. 'Just like Queen Flora. He didn't stand a chance.'

***

High above them the tornado re-materialised in a richly furnished bedchamber and spat Morag onto a polar bear rug in front of the fireplace. When she was no longer giddy from all the spinning, Morag looked around and realised where she had been taken.

'Mephista's room,' she said to herself. She had cleaned it often enough when she had been forced to be her maid. It had not changed a bit: the same sprawling bed with the gossamer curtains, the vast dressing table groaning under the weight of Mephista's perfumes and cosmetics, and the enormous, yawning fireplace, over which were hanging two oil paintings of a sad-looking man and woman reaching out for each other.

As Morag tried to regain her balance she heard a low growling snigger behind her. She turned to see a Klapp demon baring his yellow teeth in a hideous grin and clutching his pot belly as he chuckled, 'Oh that whirlwind trick never fails. And I thought it up myself!'

Morag scowled. 'Tanktop. I should have known. What are you doing here?' she snapped, anger rising in her throat. She was not afraid of this ugly creature. He had been in the Klapp Demon Secret Police, but she knew what a coward he was.

'I could ask you the same, little miss,' he replied. 'Why were you creeping and crawling about in the castle? You were looking for the prisoner, weren't you?'

Morag flinched.

'I thought so,' the Klapp demon smirked. 'My Lady will reward old Tanktop well for capturing you,' he added, rubbing his hands together. His mean little eyes gleamed. 'I wonder what I will get for the likes of you! Hmmm, Rotten Ruk Tails would be good or Sorrow Slime or...or...'

Morag closed her eyes in disgust as globules of saliva oozed from his wide mouth and leaked all over his matted chest hair. When he saw her discomfort he laughed all the more. He loped towards the door and yanked the big metal key from the lock.

'See this?' he said, waggling it at her. 'Now don't you be thinking you can escape from here, 'cos I'm going to lock you up. Do you hear?'

She nodded. His eyes flickered amber in the firelight. 'And don't be thinking your friends can come and help you either. You can forget about seeing them again.'

The Klapp demon yanked the door open.

'Wait!' cried Morag. 'Why did you do it?'

He frowned.

'The whirlwind...why did you...?' she went on, but was interrupted.

'Well, it was fun and I got to use magic. I've never been allowed to do that before...' he said, his voice high with excitement.

'No, that's not what I meant,' she replied. 'Why did you kill the Queen?'

The creature shrugged. 'She was no use any more,' he said matter-of-factly. 'My mistress had the tooth so she didn't need Flora any more. The Queen was a liability, she knew too much...Wait a minute, why am I telling you this? It's *nothing* to do with you,' he growled.

'No use to you any more? You mean the Queen *helped* you get the tooth?' Morag asked, not quite believing what she had heard.

Tanktop stared at her, unwilling to talk. 'Got to go,' he said finally and pulled the door shut. Morag waited until she heard the key scrape in the lock and felt under her coat for the medallion. 'Did you hear that?' she said. 'Henry, you've got to use your magic to get us out. I don't want to be here when he gets back...'

She put her hand to her throat and gasped. The medallion was missing! Her stomach lurched. He must have fallen off in the stairwell. She looked around. *Maybe there's another way out of here*, she thought going to the windows. She pressed her face up against the diamond panes and looked out. Through the gloom of the early winter's evening, she could just make out the cobbled courtyard a long way below, but it was too far to jump. *Not that way then*, she said to herself. She felt along the walls for signs of secret doorways, but there were no hidden catches or sliding panels. She lifted the bearskin rug and looked under the bed for a trapdoor; she peered into a large chest in the corner and knocked on the walls. After about ten minutes, it became obvious that the locked door was the only way in and out of the room. She tried not to cry, but sighed loudly and threw herself on the bed. *Now what Morag?*

A log crackled and spat on the fire. *The fire-*

place! Of course! In books she had read, the hero or heroine always found a secret passageway behind the fireplace. She leapt to her feet and ran across the room. Placing her hands carefully on the stone mantel, she searched for a button concealed in the intricate carvings, pushing and kneading the knots and stone flowers as she went. She found nothing.

'Ggnnnhh!' she said in frustration. She dropped onto the hearthrug with frustration.

'Oh poor soul...' said a man's voice from above her. Morag looked up, but could see no-one. 'It's heartbreaking watching her trying to find a way out,' it continued.

'Hello?' Morag said quietly.

'I wish we could do something for her,' said a woman's voice now. 'Like show her a way to escape. But how can we?'

'I don't think there's anything we can do, darling,' replied the man's voice. 'Not in our current position. It's so frustrating.'

Morag stood and scanned the room. There was no-one.

'Hello?' she tried again. 'Who's there?'

'Poor child. I wonder what she's done to deserve this,' said the woman sadly. 'Oh wait, isn't she the one who was here before?'

'Hmm...she could be. I always wondered what happened to her,' the man's voice replied.

'Are you ghosts?' said Morag. 'It's fine if you are. I'm not frightened. Moira and Jermy always said they had ghosts in their basement...'

'Is she talking to us?' asked the man.

'I'm not sure,' replied the woman. 'She's not supposed to be able to hear us. Mephista made sure no-one could talk to us, remember?'

'I certainly can hear you, but I can't see you!' said Morag, trying hard to keep the fear from her voice. 'Where are you? Show yourselves!'

'Bless my soul. She *can* hear us!' said the woman. 'Talk to her Nathan, ask her a question.'

'Um...hello there, little one,' Nathan said.

'Where are you?' Morag asked again.

'Turn around,' instructed the man.

Morag did. She was now facing the fireplace. She looked in the grate and up the chimney. 'Are you up there?'

'No. Do you see the two portraits above the fireplace?' he asked.

'Yes.'

'Well, that's us!' he said.

Morag raised her eyes to the two oil paintings: one was of a man with dark brown hair, the other of a blond woman wearing a red stone pendant. 'But...I don't understand,' she said. 'How can I hear you speak when you're not moving?'

'That's a good question, my dear. Most people can't,' said the woman softly. 'Are you using magic? Mephista's entrapment spell was very powerful. She made sure no one could hear us or help us to escape. Are you a witch?'

'No, I'm not a witch at all,' replied Morag. 'I'm

just an ordinary human girl.'

'A human child?' asked the woman with surprise. 'Yet you can *hear* us? How can that be, Nathan?'

'Maybe Mephista's spell is wearing off? It doesn't matter. It's a miracle that after all this time someone can hear us. Perhaps now we can be freed...' the man said with real hope in his voice.

There was a pause. Morag, who was bursting with questions, asked: 'Why did Mephista trap you in the paintings? I've met her before and that is cruel, even for her. What did you do?'

'We fell in love,' Nathan explained. 'Mephista didn't like it, tracked us down and imprisoned us in these pictures.'

'But *why* would she do that?' the girl asked. 'Why was she so against you falling in love?'

'It's a bit complicated,' he replied. 'Isabella and I are both heirs to the Marnoch Mor crown. Look, it's a long story and it will take some time to tell it all...' Nathan stopped suddenly. 'What was that?'

There was a scuffling at the door, a key turned and the scraggy face of Tanktop leered in at Morag. 'You're to come with me,' he said with a nasty grin.

Morag flinched. 'I'm not going *anywhere*,' she said bravely, although she wasn't feeling in the least bit brave.

'Atta girl!' Nathan cheered her on, knowing

only Morag would hear him.

The Klapp demon scowled, grabbed her tightly by the arms and dragged her towards the door. Morag pulled and twisted and turned and punched and kicked, and did everything she could to loosen the creature's grip, but it was no use. Tanktop had her and he was not letting go. There was nothing she could do but go with him.

She allowed herself the briefest glance back at the paintings. *I don't know how, but somehow I'll help you*, she thought as she was pulled through the doorway and into the corridor beyond. Even though she knew the figures in the paintings could not move, their faces seemed sadder than ever.

chapter thirteen

'Move it, human!'

Tanktop growled and gave Morag a harsh tug, pulling her off her feet. She stumbled and nearly fell as he dragged her downstairs. Morag tried to keep up with him, but the Klapp demon struck up such a pace, that it was impossible not to fall behind.

'Slow down,' she pleaded, nearly tumbling down the stairwell. 'We don't all move like Klapp demons you know!'

'Stop whining!' he said with a snarl. 'You're wanted and you're wanted now!'

'Who wants me?'

'You'll find out soon enough,' he snorted.

Without stopping, Tanktop dragged her to the top of the stairwell that led down to the dungeon. He wasted no time in scampering ahead, his great feet slapping hard on the steps as he pulled her behind. Deciding she'd had quite enough of this treatment, Morag suddenly let her body relax and slid to the floor. Tanktop was abruptly yanked off his feet and hit the stairs with a yowl. He scrambled to his feet and turned on her, spit flying from his lips in rage. 'What are you doing, stupid girl?' he hissed, slapping her shoulder. 'Get up! Get up!'

But Morag stayed put, staring back defiantly. 'Let me go,' she said. 'I've done nothing wrong.'

'Oh, but you have. You broke into this castle illegally,' the Klapp demon smiled smugly. He was pleased with his good answer. 'You're not supposed to be here. You've got a nerve coming back to this island after what you did to Devlish.'

'You should be thanking me for getting rid of him,' she began, but got no further for the Klapp demon grabbed her by the waist and threw her over his shoulder.

'Let me go!' she squealed as he carried her down the stairs. She wriggled and kicked, but his grip was too tight for her to break, and it became apparent that all her struggling was getting her nowhere. With a sigh, Morag had no choice but to allow herself to be carried into the dungeon.

Despite his gangly frame, Tanktop negotiated the twists with agility. At the bottom of the stairs was a wooden door. Tanktop flipped his prisoner from his shoulder and dropped her unceremoniously onto the floor. While he examined the large iron lock, Morag wondered if now was a good time to try to escape. Eyes pinned to the Klapp demon, she slowly edged aside. She took another step, then another and then...

'Ow!' she cried as his sharp nails dug into her shoulder and he dragged her close to his face.

'You're going nowhere. Even if you tried to run I'd catch you,' he growled, teeth bared and eyes glinting in the torchlight. She recoiled from his horrible breath.

'Get your hands off me,' she said, slapping his grasping fingers. 'When everyone in Marnoch Mor hears about this, *they'll* be the ones who come after *you!'*

He stared at her for a few seconds, then grunted and, keeping a secure hold of her, produced a small wand, seemingly from nowhere. He pointed it at the door, called out a dark Klapp demon magic spell and a stream of purple sparks flew at the lock. There was a small click, the handle turned and the door swung open with a high-pitched shriek. Morag flinched as she found herself being wrenched through the doorway into the darkness beyond.

The door banged shut behind her. She was aware of the Klapp demon's snuffles, and could feel a dirt floor beneath her feet, but could not see it. She believed they had entered a narrow corridor, but she could not be sure. There was nothing to guide them, no torches on the walls, no chinks of light at all. The demon, undeterred by the pitch blackness all around, continued dragging her onwards and Morag could do nothing but follow. As she stumbled along, she wondered if her friends had managed to escape and if they were looking for her. She wondered what had happened to Henry and hoped Aldiss and Bertie had the sense to get out of the castle altogether and fetch Shona. Now that she had been captured, they hadn't a hope of rescuing Montgomery.

'You won't get away with this,' she said, finally finding her voice again. 'My friends from Marnoch Mor will come and rescue me.'

'Ha!' laughed the demon, not slowing his pace. 'They won't be able to if there's no Marnoch Mor left...'

'They will, you know, and then you'll be sorry. I'll tell them everything: how you kidnapped Montgomery and murdered the Queen and then held me hostage and...'

But she got no further. Tanktop suddenly stopped, causing her to crash into him.

'What are you doing...?' she demanded.

There was a flash as the wand was lit. More purple sparks poured from its tip like a sparkler on Bonfire Night. The demon barked some magic words, and a doorway opened up in the darkness, flooding the passageway with a bright light. Morag shielded her eyes with an arm and recoiled. 'Mistress, look what I bring you,' Tanktop hissed as he pushed Morag in front of him.

Morag blinked, her eyes watering in the bright light. A strong smell of decay made her wrinkle her nose in disgust.

'Well! Look who it is,' a familiar voice said.

As her eyes grew accustomed to the brightness, she saw with horror who had spoken. A tall slender woman was staring down at her.

'Well done, Tanktop, you'll be rewarded later,'

said Mephista, daughter of the evil warlock Devlish, as a nasty smile played about her lips. Morag's heart beat wildly, and she could only stare at Mephista. She had hoped never to meet her again.

The witch looked magnificent in a long silk dress of palest blue, her red hair flowing down her back like a river of fire. Around her throat, dangling from a long gold chain was a human tooth, an incisor. *The tooth that was stolen from the museum!* Morag realised. It swung as the witch laughed in the face of the frightened girl standing before her.

'You didn't expect to see *me* again, did you?' the witch smirked.

'Where is Montgomery?' Morag demanded. 'What have you done with him?'

Mephista's lips pursed before she answered. 'Your concern is so sweet, and so predictable. And you wouldn't want anyone to harm him, now would you?'

Mephista glanced behind her and for the first time Morag realised a figure was slumped in a dark corner. She squinted in the gloom and could just make out a familiar face. '*Montgomery?* Let him go! You have no reason to lock him up like this!' Morag shouted, straining to free herself from Tanktop's grip. The demon cackled and held on tightly.

'Ah, but this was the only way,' replied Mephista. 'You left me no choice.'

'What do you mean?'

The witch strode towards her and bent down so that their noses were almost touching.

'I knew that in order to get you to leave Marnoch Mor, I'd have to tempt you out. I couldn't get you out using magic but if you chose to come of your own accord...now that would be a different matter. So I took your precious Montgomery as bait.'

'Bait? What are you talking about?' Although Morag asked the question, she already knew the answer and the realisation made her feel sick.

'Bait for you. The great Morag MacTavish, heroine of Marnoch Mor and *murderer* of my father,' Mephsita snarled.

'I did *not* murder your father,' Morag said calmly. 'The Eye of Lornish did it...'

'Oh you can blame the Eye, but it was you all right and now that I've got you here you're going to pay for what you did.'

Mephista smirked, stood back and strolled away.

'Whatever you're going to do to me,' Morag pleaded, 'at least let Montgomery go.'

The witch waved an arm and a section of the room, previously shrouded in darkness, was suddenly lit by three large Full Moonstones set into the wall. Morag gasped. There, lying on a white marble table was a body covered from head to toe by a shroud. Standing behind it was a large four-armed Girallon, whom Mephista introduced as Kang. Beside the table was a wooden trolley laden with various objects including a jade bowl, a glittering dagger and a large dusty spell book. Mephista lifted the dagger and, turning back to Morag, stroked it gently.

'Oh, I'm not going to kill you,' she said. 'Not yet anyway. No, you're more important to me alive.' She turned to Tanktop. 'Get her ready.'

Tanktop chuckled as Morag pulled and twisted against him and ignored her kicks and screams as he tied her to a stone pillar. When he was finished, Morag could not move her legs or her left arm. Her right arm had been left free and she used it to swipe at the cackling Klapp demon.

'Let me go!' Morag screamed as she struggled against her bonds. 'Let me go, Mephista, or you'll be sorry!'

Mephista, who had been making preparations for whatever she had in mind, was bemused by Morag's outburst.

'What are you going to do? Take me to prison in your little fairy kingdom? You and I know that's never going to happen. In any case, very soon Marnoch Mor will be destroyed. Even as we speak that place is imploding.'

She pointed to a round Moonstone on a stand. When Morag looked closely she saw it was flickering, and the flickers looked like people and animals and buildings. The people and animals were running, crying, falling, and the buildings were tearing themselves apart and collapsing into piles of rubble.

'I don't know how, but Marnoch Mor and Montgomery are somehow linked,' Mephista went on. 'When we captured him, the town began to fall apart. One seems not to be able to survive without the other. How *delicious* is that? Not only do I get to destroy you, but that place as well and all the goody two-shoes who live there!'

Morag watched helplessly as the witch strode to where Montgomery lay and crouched beside him. She grabbed his hair and pulled his head back. Morag was horrified to see how swollen and bloody it was.

'It took me some time to get the right information out of him, but he told me...eventually.' She let Montgomery's hair go and his head banged off the stone floor with a sickening bump. Mephista stood up and swept over to the collection of objects.

'Let him go,' Morag pleaded. 'Please. Do what you will with me, but let him go.'

'How very noble of you, my dear,' said the witch, taking up the dagger again with the jade bowl, 'but it's too late. You see, after I've taken what I need from you, you and your friend over there will be disposed of and there's nothing you can do or say that will change my mind. I'll be glad to get rid of you both.'

'You will pay for this, Mephista!' the girl raged. 'I have friends and they'll come and get you!'

The witch laughed and raised the dagger.

chapter fourteen

Morag's heart missed a beat as the witch bore down on her. She could not tear her eyes away from the knife that glittered menacingly in Mephista's hand. The witch smirked as she drew closer, pleasure gleaming in her eyes. Morag's breath quickened and she fought to control it.

'What are you doing?' Morag's voice sounded small and far away.

'I'm taking back something you took from me,' the witch replied. She nodded to Tanktop. 'Hold her still while I make the cut.'

Morag struggled even more, but she was bound tight. She tried to pull away her free hand when Tanktop gripped her wrist. The creature laughed as he twisted her arm round to expose her wrist which glowed white in the light from the Moonstones. It was all too easy to see where a knife wound could make the most impact. She looked around desperately for someone to help her, but apart from the unconscious Montgomery, there was no-one. Even Henry was gone.

'Montgomery!' she called as Mephista raised the dagger above her head and began to chant an incantation.

'Montgomery!' she screamed again as Mephista

stopped chanting and brought the dagger down to her arm. Morag looked away, screwing up her eyes. Then...nothing.

She opened her eyes.

She could feel the cold steel against her skin. Fearful, but trying not to whimper, Morag watched as the witch drew the blade across her wrist. Tiny beads of scarlet immediately burst forth and the last thing Morag felt was the spreading burn of pain. She blacked out.

When Morag came round again Mephista was pouring something into the little jade bowl. Wincing, Morag looked at her throbbing arm and saw a two inch slash. Blood was oozing out and dripping to the floor. She pulled her arm to her side, smearing blood all over her coat as she made a feeble attempt to stem the flow.

The witch smiled when she saw the girl had wakened.

'Ah Morag, so glad you could join us for the main event,' she sneered. 'Watch as I say the final words that will bring *him* back to me, and restore the true ruler of Murst. You had the *one* vital ingredient I needed.'

'I did? I don't understand...'

'Your blood. It was the one thing missing from the spell. Without it, I couldn't complete it.'

She carried the jade bowl over to the body under the shroud. In one sweeping motion she pulled the covering off, causing Morag to gasp. For lying there, ghastly pale and shrivelled, was the body of Devlish. Mephista stroked his cold, pinched face.

'I needed the blood of the one who killed him,' the witch said as she prised open her father's mouth and carefully poured the contents down his throat.

She whispered the last magic words and gently closed the dead man's mouth. She passed the bowl to Kang, stood back and watched. Silence fell on the room as everyone waited to see what would happen next. Morag too, horrified and fascinated at the same time, could not keep herself from staring at the dead warlock.

But nothing happened.

Mephista frowned. She looked questioningly at Kang and Tanktop, but they looked back at her blankly. She turned to her father's body again. 'Tanktop, you promised me this would work!' were the only words the witch managed before she noticed a strange look on the Klapp demon's face. Tanktop was staring at his master, opening and closing his large mouth like a fish out of water. He pointed to Devlish. Mephista turned to look, her eyes shining with hope as she saw Devlish blink. She ran to his side, slipped an arm under his and helped him sit up.

'Father!' Her voice was breathless and full of emotion, 'You've come back to me. You're alive.'

The warlock closed his eyes, body swaying. He opened them again and looked around. Frowning, he stared at her as if he were trying to work out who she was.

'Don't you recognise me, Father?' she asked.

The warlock stared beyond her, caught sight of Kang's smirk and nodded, then looked back at Mephista. 'Of course I know you, my daughter,' he smiled.

That was enough to reassure Mephista. She turned and gave Morag a triumphant look. 'Kang,' she said, not taking her eyes off Morag, 'help my father to his feet and take him to his quarters. He'll need rest. Tanktop, get rid of the girl.'

'What does your Ladyship want me to do with her?'

'I don't care. Throw her to the wolves, throw her in the sea like that other maid, anything. Just make sure she never troubles me again.'

The demon bowed. 'And the wizard, my Lady?' he asked, indicating with his thumb to where Montgomery still lay.

'I haven't finished with him. Take him up to my room.'

Tanktop bowed low as Mephista followed Kang and the newly risen Devlish into the corridor. 'Throw her to the wolves, she says, throw her to the snarling, biting wolves!' he muttered to himself as soon as they were gone. 'And how does she think I'm going to do that without getting eaten myself?'

'You could just take me to the edge of the forest. Leave me there for the wolves,' Morag suggested. 'She'd never know. And *I* won't tell her.'

The demon strode over and peered closely into her face. The stench from his breath was overpowering and Morag, already sickened by what she had seen moments earlier, was forced to pull away.

'My Lady is expecting you to die,' he said matter-of-factly. 'I cannot disobey her.'

'You can't kill me,' she said as he began to untie her. 'Not after my friends saved your life.'

The demon frowned at her.

'Your friends saved *me*?'

'Don't you remember? A few months ago when you were in Kyle's boat and we caught you trying to steal Bertie's satchel?'

The demon nodded.

'My friends didn't kill you then. They even fed you your favourite food. So you shouldn't kill me now. One good turn deserves another?' Morag tried hopefully.

Tanktop thought about this for a moment. The girl was right: he had been treated fairly well by her friends. On the other hand, her Ladyship was good to him too. She hadn't turned him into anything nasty yet—unlike his Uncle Bobble-hat, whom Mephista had transformed into a lit candle after she overheard him telling a joke about her. His mother never had managed to get the wax out of the carpet.

'No, I cannot let you go,' he said, shaking the rope from the girl's body. 'I must obey my Ladyship. She'd turn me into a fork or a door-handle or something worse if she found out I'd let you go.'

With a large bony hand tightly gripping her shoulder, Tanktop led the protesting girl out of the dungeon. As Morag left she glanced regretfully at Montgomery lying on the cold dank floor. Her heart sank. She had come to save him, but now she was the one who needed saving. She wished she could do something for him, but the demon shoved her on insistently.

'You're not really going to leave me for the wolves, are you?' she ventured as she was marched up the stairs. She knew the Klapp demon was a horrible, spiteful creature, but surely even he wouldn't stoop so low as to kill her in cold blood? Then she remembered Queen Flora and the dart that killed her, and Tanktop's words that the Queen had been 'of no use any more'. She baulked. Mephista had used her for her blood and now *she* was of no further use. Why would the demon treat her any differently?

As he kicked open the door at the top of the landing and shoved her through, she desperately tried to conjure something that would stop him in his tracks, but she was too terrified to think clearly. She was bundled into the dark corridor, past a huge tapestry depicting the gigantic figure of Devlish crushing Marnoch Mor beneath his feet.

It was then that she heard a loud clunk, a small whimper and the *whump* of a body hitting the flagstone floor.

She spun around to find Tanktop lying uncon-scious on the ground. He was not moving.

'I've wanted to do that for ages,' a voice in the darkness said.

Chelsea stepped into the light and stood over the demon, a heavy silver candlestick in her hand. 'He's one of the really nasty ones. Sneaky little...'

'Chelsea! Am *I* glad to see you,' Morag cried. 'But where are the others? Aren't Shona, Bertie and Aldiss with you?'

'I've got them hiding in the woods,' replied the girl. 'I had to come back to get a cure for...' She paused, for the news was not good. 'It's Aldiss...' she began.

'What about him? *Is he all right?*' Morag grabbed the girl as if about to shake the information from her.

'No, he's not,' Chelsea told her. 'He was hit by a poisoned dart. He's very ill. If we don't do some-thing, he'll die.'

'Where is he? Take me to him!' she urged, for-getting all about Montgomery.

***

It was easy to sneak back outside. They ran out the side door and straight to a little clearing a few metres into the wood. Shona and Bertie raced to greet Morag, but all the girl could think of was her rat friend and she batted away their questions. 'Where is he?' she asked, searching the ground.

'We've laid him down here,' Shona said, stepping aside to reveal Aldiss lying on a bed of bracken. Morag kneeled by him and placed her hand on his shivering body. The little rat, whiskers quivering with fever, opened his eyes briefly and then fell back into a deep sleep. 'He needs a doctor,' Morag said. 'We need to get him home.'

Shona shook her head, her yellow eyes full of sorrow. 'By the time we get him back to the mainland it'll be too late for him, Morag,' she said emotionally.

'He's dying,' Bertie whispered.

'No!' Morag sobbed. 'There must be something we can do for him!' She looked from Shona to Bertie and back again. 'We can't give up on him!'

Bertie and Shona hung their heads and a large tear trickled down Bertie's feathered face. Morag couldn't believe it. Aldiss *couldn't* be dying. That was unthinkable. Stroking his little head, she frantically thought of what they should do next, but her mind was a blank.

'What about your bag?' she asked the dodo tearfully. 'It can make any food you ask for. Couldn't it come up with something?'

'We've tried that,' he replied. 'It didn't work... the forest...it interferes with magic just as Ivy said.'

'What does Henry think? Surely he could help?'

Bertie looked at Shona, who looked at Morag.

'We were rather hoping you'd tell us that,' said Bertie.

'Isn't he with you?' Shona asked.

'No, he came off when I was sucked into that whirlwind,' Morag replied. She stood up. 'He must still be in the castle. Chelsea, I need you to get me back inside.'

'Forget it, Morag,' said Shona. 'It's too dangerous.'

'And there won't be enough time,' added Bertie sadly. 'What if you're caught? We'll lose Aldiss *and* you.'

Morag was insistent. 'I don't care. I'm going back. I *must* find Henry. He's the only one who can save Aldiss now. In any case, Montgomery's still in there.'

***

Morag and Chelsea crept along the corridor until they found the door that led down to the dungeons. Tanktop was no longer lying on the ground and Morag's heart skipped a beat when she realised that he was probably looking for her right now. She opened the door and quickly pulled Chelsea inside.

Together the girls ran until they reached the foot of the stairwell where Morag had been attacked by Tanktop's tornado. She cursed herself for not bringing a Moonstone as it was as dark as a coal cellar and therefore difficult to see anything on the ground.

'Henry,' she called in a loud whisper. 'Are you here? Henry? Hello!'

She felt across the cold flagstones for any sign of the medallion, but could not find him anywhere. She climbed up and down the stairs several times, and asked Chelsea to look as well, but eventually Morag had to accept that Henry was not there. She sat down on the steps and thought over the events that led up to her being taken. She had felt herself being sucked up into the vortex, when Aldiss had grabbed Henry and tried to pull her down. The wind had picked up, and she had felt the chain scraping across her neck, Henry slipping over her head, into the air and...

'He got caught round a torch!' she remembered excitedly.

There were three nearby, all looking as if they were leaning over to get a better view of whoever might come down the stairs. They flickered in the draughts that swept up and down the stairwell, sending Morag and Chelsea's shadows dancing on the walls behind them. Morag peered up at the one closest to her. Then she smiled. There, twisted around the metal sconce was the unmistakable glitter of Henry's chain, and propped up against the sparking oil torch was the medallion himself.

'Kneel down,' Morag urged Chelsea, who frowned.

'What? Why?'

'I can't reach him. I need to climb up on you to get closer.'

Grumbling, Chelsea did as she was asked, and felt Morag put a foot on her back and then, with a rocking motion, heave herself up. Standing unsteadily, Morag stretched up and grabbed the chain. She untangled it and pulled until it was loosened. Henry came flying down and would have hit her on the face had she not quickly ducked out of the way. With a triumphant cry of 'Yes!' Morag leapt to the stairs and helped Chelsea to her feet.

They both peered at Henry.

'What's wrong with him?' Chelsea asked. 'Why are his eyes closed?'

'He must have been knocked out when he fell off my neck,' said Morag. 'Poor Henry...'

'Ooooh!' said Henry, coming round. 'Where am I? When is this? Who are you? You're not Magma...'

His tiny eyes flickered open and he stared up at the girls, disdain washing over his face. He grimaced. 'I don't like girls,' he added with a snort.

Morag rolled her eyes. 'Henry, it's me, Morag. We're in Murst Castle. We've come to rescue Montgomery,' she said. 'Except that something worse has happened.'

'Worse? What's worse than being in this horrible place?' the medallion complained.

'Oh Henry, it's all gone wrong. Montgomery is still trapped, Aldiss has been injured and is probably dying, and...Mephista has brought Devlish back to life,' she added quickly.

Chelsea gawped. 'You never told me *that* when you brought me back in here,' she said. 'If I had known *that* I wouldn't have come.'

'I just wanted to get in here, find Montgomery and Henry and leave,' Morag said. 'Henry, you must help us. Aldiss was hit by a poisonous dart, the same kind that killed Queen Flora. If we don't do something, he'll die.'

'Who's Aldiss?' asked the medallion.

'The rat!' Chelsea hissed.

'I know a rat? How odd...' he replied.

'Henry, please! Try to remember, it's important. Aldiss is sick. You've got to help him, there's no one else we can ask,' said Morag, close to tears.

'I don't think I can help you,' replied the medallion flatly. 'I don't even know who I am let alone having to help some strange rat with a poison dart.'

And then he began to hum to himself a merry little tune that Morag found extremely irritating in the circumstances. It was Chelsea who acted. She grabbed the medallion from Morag's hand, swung him by the chain and slammed him against the wall.

'Chelsea!' Morag cried.

'Ow! What did you do that for?' Henry screamed.

'What? He must have lost his memory when he hit his head. Bash him again and he'll get it back. It's a medical fact,' said Chelsea huffily.

'Are you all right, Henry?' Morag asked. 'Do you know who I am?'

'Of course I know who you are,' he snapped. He was in a dangerous mood now he was back to his old self.

'So can you help Aldiss?'

'No,' said the medallion.

'Do you know who *can* help?'

'No, I don't.'

'Can you help at all?' asked Chelsea. 'Or are you just jewellery now?'

'Yes,' he said haughtily. 'I mean no!'

'Well?' both girls said at once.

The medallion, who liked a bit of drama, looked from one to the other, taking his time and relishing the tension.

'The tooth,' he finally said. 'You'll need Mina's tooth. It's the only thing strong enough to work in the forest and reverse the poison used by the Klapp demons.'

Morag and Chelsea looked at each other in horror.

'Does he need another bash on the head or do you have any idea what he's talking about?' Chelsea asked.

'Yes, unfortunately it makes perfect sense,' said Morag.

'And do you know where this tooth is?'

'Yes, I've seen it,' she replied. 'It's hanging around Mephista's neck.'

chapter fifteen

Henry whined about his aching head all the way to the dungeon. Morag stuck him in her pocket beside her parents' book, so his complaints were easier to ignore. Chelsea had to get back to her work before she was missed by the other staff, so said her goodbyes and disappeared, leaving Morag alone in the gloomy stairwell. Morag was not looking forward to returning to the depths of the castle where Devlish had been brought back to life, but her concern for Montgomery and Aldiss drove her on.

The door into the dungeon was still open when she approached. 'Someone's still down here,' she whispered to herself more than to Henry. Quietly, she crept towards it and peeked through the gap.

The dungeon was dim and at first Morag thought it was empty. As her eyes grew accustomed to the bluish light of the Moonstones, she noticed the body of Montgomery still lying on the floor. Her first urge was to rush to him, but she held back, staying behind the door in case whoever had opened it was still there.

Just then, the ugly face of Tanktop appeared from behind a pillar. He had wrapped a bandage around his head in a higgledy-piggledy fashion, leaving the ends loose over his large ears. He snorted and snuffled then turned his attention to the wizard.

'So, the little brat got away. You won't be so lucky, mister,' he cackled. 'Nope, my mistress has great plans for you.'

He loped over to Montgomery, bent down and heaved him up on to his feet. Growling and moaning, Tanktop dragged him over to the door. Morag pulled back and flattened herself in the shadows. She heard the demon curse and then another *whump* of a body hitting the floor. Unfortunately this time it wasn't Tanktop's.

'You are too big an' heavy for the likes of me to carry all the way up them stairs,' the demon growled. There was a pause before he continued: 'She'll not know if I magic you out of that slumber and put you back when I get you upstairs.'

Morag heard the pat of his feet on the floor as he came closer. Through the crack in the door she saw Tanktop waving a stick with two prongs at Montgomery. He spoke a few magic words, brought the wand down and sent bolts exploding from the tips, hitting Montgomery square in the chest. The wizard jolted, twitched and convulsed. From her hiding place, Morag could only watch helplessly. Then something wonderful happened; the twitching stopped and Montgomery took a deep breath and opened his eyes. He blinked, yawned, looked around him and sat up.

'What…what happened?' he asked sleepily.

'Hee-hee…Who says a Klapp demon can't do magic?' Tanktop cackled, clapping his hands in delight.

'What am I doing here?' Montgomery frowned at the stinking creature as he scrambled to his feet.

'You're our prisoner and you'll come with me.' The demon grinned manically. His eyes were bulging, and his sharp teeth were glinting in the half light.

'I'll do no such thing!' Montgomery snapped.

'I wasn't *asking* you, I was *telling* you!' Tanktop snarled, waving the wand in Montgomery's face, causing it to spark and spit. Morag knew when a Klapp demon's eyes narrowed to slits he meant business. The wizard was not carrying a wand of his own so he had no way to defend himself if Tanktop turned nasty again. Morag could not just stand back and see him dragged off again. Swallowing nervously, she took a deep breath and did the only thing she could. She jumped into the chamber and shouted at the top of her voice: 'He's not going anywhere!'

Tanktop spun round, surprised. His eyes narrowed still further when he saw Morag. He ignored Montgomery for a moment and aimed his wand at her instead.

'You…' he growled. 'You smacked me on the head!'

'No, I didn't,' she began, 'but that's neither here

nor there. You *will* let Montgomery go and you will do it now!'

She used her most commanding voice, hearing the words echo off the walls. Tanktop's mouth split into a wide grin and he began to laugh. He laughed until he had to hug his sides. Tears rolled down his greasy cheeks and he let out great guffaws, sending out clouds of pungent Klapp demon breath. Morag held her nose.

'You think you can tell me what to do? You—a weak little human girl! I wouldn't even need my magic to dispatch something like you,' he said, producing his blow pipe from nowhere. 'What could you do to me? You have nobody, and you have nothing.'

'That's where you're wrong,' Morag replied. 'I have this!' She held up Henry, so that the light from the Moonstones flashed off the diamonds that circled his face.

The demon shrugged. 'Tsk! A mere bauble,' he sneered.

'I am NOT A BAUBLE!' snapped Henry, and in an instant all the Moonstones went *Blink!* and the room was plunged into darkness. Morag's eyes took a few seconds to adjust but she saw the demon was standing stock-still. He was not breathing or moving. As she looked more closely she could see he had been frozen. She held Henry up to her face.

'What have you done?' she demanded.

'I am *not* a bauble,' he said meekly.

'Turn him back!'

'I can't. That spell can't be reversed, but don't worry it'll wear off in a few hours,' he said sullenly. 'He's better out of our way. Horrible sneaking, stinking thing that he is.'

'Henry's right, Morag,' Montgomery said, side-stepping the demon. 'We can't let him raise the alarm.'

She nodded, then a smile spread over her face and tears of joy sprang to her eyes. She ran to Montgomery and gave him a hug. 'I am so glad you're all right,' she said. 'I was so worried.'

Montgomery hugged her back. 'I'm fine, no bones broken,' he assured her, 'although...I'm not sure exactly what happened. The last thing I remember is being in my office back home.'

'Mephista had you whisked over to Murst in a whirlwind. Marnoch Mor is falling apart without you.' She hesitated, to gulp back her tears.

Montgomery was stunned.

'We—Shona, Bertie, Aldiss, Henry and me— knew we had to find you. Only, when we got here it turned out Mephista was after *me*, not you.'

The wizard listened intently. 'You? For revenge?'

'No. She took my blood. She said she needed it as the final part of the spell to bring Devlish back to life.'

'What? She cannot do that!' blurted Montgomery. 'Oh, this is terrible. No-one has the authority to bring the dead back to life. It's been prohibited by the WWWC for as long as I can remember. When someone dies we must let them go.'

Morag's lip trembled and her eyes filled with tears. 'Well it's too late now, he's back. And Aldiss is dying too. Right now! And I know he's only a rat but he's brave and he's my friend. And the only thing that might help is the tooth Mephista is wearing around her neck.'

Montgomery placed a hand on her shoulder and smiled. 'Then what are we waiting for?'

***

Although the castle was vast, Mephista was not difficult to find. Her shrill and angry voice reached Morag and Montgomery by the time they got to the corridor by the Great Hall. Morag put her fingers to her lips and pointed towards the throne room. The door was open just wide enough to offer a view of the witch on her throne. Morag could see that Mephista had something around her neck, but wasn't sure if it was the tooth. She squinted to get a better look. Seconds passed, a minute.

'Well?' whispered Montgomery.

'She's not wearing it,' said Morag. 'It must be in her room. Come on, let's go.'

They raced to the staircase that led to the sleeping quarters. In spite of her tiredness, the girl leapt two stairs at a time, her stomach churning with dread that they wouldn't find the tooth in time. The memory of Aldiss's little whiskered face swam in her mind but she pushed it away. They climbed until they reached the floor of Mephista's grand bedroom.

'Wait here,' Morag whispered on the landing.

Body flat against the cold stone wall and breathing as lightly as she could, she peered around the entranceway into a corridor of doors.

Empty. There was no-one in sight. She let out a sigh of relief and was about to step out of the shadows when she heard voices from a room at the end of the corridor. She leapt back just in time as MacAndrew—warrior and Devlish's right hand man—walked out and bowed, his long shaggy hair falling over his face.

'Yes sire,' she heard him say, 'it will be attended to at once.'

The warrior, sword at his belt, bowed once more before turning on his heel and walking down the corridor towards them. Morag grabbed Montgomery by the sleeve and dragged him up another flight of stairs. They leapt onto the landing above as MacAndrew entered the stairwell. Morag and Montgomery stood still and listened as his footsteps drew closer. Morag swallowed hard and closed her eyes. *Please don't come up, please don't come up*, she prayed. The footsteps paused, then MacAndrew sighed and continued *down* the stairs.

'That was close,' she said as she checked to make sure he really had gone.

'Too close,' replied Montgomery. 'We can't risk being caught that easily.'

'Come on, let's get into that room, find the tooth and get out of here.'

***

Except for the fire that still smouldered in the hearth, Mephista's room was in shadow when they crept in. Leaving Montgomery to keep watch at the door, Morag immediately realised that finding the tooth was going to be more difficult than she had imagined. 'It could be anywhere...' she whispered to herself.

'So, you've come back,' said a voice in the darkness. 'We knew you would.'

Morag's blood froze.

From their frames above the fireplace, the portraits of Nathan and Isabella seemed to smile at her. Relieved, Morag explained about Aldiss and the tooth.

'Did you see Mephista take off a pendant and put it away?' she asked.

'She may have put something in the dressing table drawer,' Isabella replied.

Morag ran to it and began pulling out the drawers. Rummaging around in the lace and powders inside, she saw nothing that looked like a tooth. She pulled out the second and third. Nothing. There was one more to try, but when she pulled it, it didn't budge.

'It's locked!' she hissed in frustration. 'Where's the key?'

'She keeps it with her at all times,' said Nathan.

'I need to get that tooth!' growled Morag, yanking on the drawer handle. 'Aldiss will die without it.'

'Let *me* have a look,' Henry mumbled from her pocket.

Morag fished him out and held him to the lock. He closed his eyes and started to vibrate. He stopped and looked at the lock expectantly. Nothing had happened.

'Drat!' he said. 'There must be a spell that's just for furniture...'

'Come on Henry! We don't have much time!'

He kept trying until at last, on his fifth attempt, they heard the lock click and the drawer shot out, crashing to the floor and spilling its contents everywhere. Out of the jumble of jewellery and gloves flew the tooth, still attached to its gold chain. It bounced to Morag's feet. She snatched it up and ran to the door.

'We've got it!' she cried to Montgomery.

'Well done,' he told her.

They were just about to run when Morag heard Nathan's voice.

'Morag! Wait! What about us?'

'You can't leave us here.' Isabella pleaded. 'Please. You must help us.'

Morag turned to Montgomery. 'They're right,' she said. 'I can't leave them here.'

The wizard was confused. 'What do you mean? Leave who?'

'Nathan and Isabella. They're asking for our help...'

Montgomery looked back at her blankly and shook his head.

'You can't hear their voices, can you?' she asked. When she gazed at the paintings of Nathan and Isabella she saw their faces, normally rigid and unchanging, now seemed sad and hopeful all at once. Morag thrust the tooth into the wizard's hand.

'Wait here,' she said. She rushed over to the fireplace and, arms straining, lifted the large paintings off the wall.

'It's no use. You're too heavy to carry downstairs,' she admitted. Then, her eyes fell on something glittering on the dressing table. 'Of course!'

Morag ran over, grabbed a nail file and used it to slice around Nathan's frame.

'What are you doing? Come on, we need to go!' Montgomery pressed from the doorway.

Large bare feet slapped loudly on the stairs outside.

'Morag!' Montgomery's voice was insistent, urgent. 'What in the name of Colm Breck are you doing?'

'I'm coming,' she replied, hastily rolling up the painting of Nathan. 'Just one more to do...'

But Montgomery was not listening. He crept into the room and quietly closed the door behind him.

He put his fingers to his lips and froze. Someone was coming. Morag swallowed and stopped moving. The footsteps had left the stairwell and were getting louder as they came down the corridor.

Thump, thump, thump, thump.

Morag clapped a hand over her mouth to muffle her panicked breaths. There was nowhere to hide. She looked at Montgomery. He, too, was barely breathing.

Thump, thump, thump, thump.

The footsteps stopped. Morag saw the shadow of something huge under the crack of the door. That something gave the air a long and deliberate sniff. That something took a step towards the door. That something rattled the handle. It turned slowly. With a shrill squeak the door started to open...

'Kang! Is that you?' Devlish's voice rang out from further down the corridor. 'Get back here.'

Kang grunted a response, slammed the door shut again and stomped off down the corridor towards the warlock's room. Montgomery closed his eyes and slumped against the door. It took Morag a few moments to compose herself enough to return to cutting out Isabella's painting. As she did this, Montgomery opened the door a crack to listen.

'Thank you for rescuing us,' Isabella said as Morag gently lifted her out of her frame.

'No problem,' she replied. 'I'll take you back to Marnoch Mor and I'm sure someone there will break the spell and free you.'

'I hope so,' replied Isabella, her voice muffled and sounding faraway.

Morag rolled up the painting and secured both with black ribbon from Mephista's dressing table. Tucking them under her arm she ran to Montgomery's side.

'I'm ready.'

'Just a minute,' he replied.

The wizard stood for some moments at the door, listening to raised voices coming from Devlish's room.

'It sounds like Devlish and Kang,' he said.

Morag stood behind him, and stuck her ear against the door.

'You promised me this body would be in better condition, Kang!' snapped Devlish. 'Look at it! It's decaying. I feel so weak. Couldn't you have found me a better body?'

'When I heard Mephista wanted to resurrect her father,' explained Kang, 'I offered my services right away. It was the only way I could bring my Great Master over from the dark side.'

'Why did you not bring me back sooner?'

'It took us longer than expected to acquire the necessary items, sire,' the Girallon replied. 'That girl was especially hard to take from Marnoch Mor. They were watching her all the time, so we had to use *other* methods to lure her out. That fool Klapp demon thinks he was behind it all, but if it hadn't been for me teaching him how to use magic...'

'And what happened to the tooth?' the warlock growled.

'The witch still has it,' replied Kang, 'but don't worry, I shall be taking it from her tonight. Once you are strong enough, Oh Great Amergin, we will fulfil the other part of our plan. Mephista won't know what's hit her.'

'And neither will Marnoch Mor!' cackled the other voice.

'*Amergin*?' Morag whispered to Montgomery. 'I thought he was talking to Devlish.'

She searched the wizard's face for an explanation.

'Oh dear. This is much worse than I thought,' he said, frowning. 'Kang has double-crossed Mephista and Tanktop. They haven't brought Devlish back to life at all. Amergin has possessed him. And he and Kang are going to seize power from Mephista.'

'Who is Amergin? You know, don't you?'

Montgomery bowed his head, his face white and tense. When he heard a sudden movement from Devlish's room he quickly closed the door.

'They're coming,' he whispered, shoving Morag away. 'Quick, hide behind the bed!'

They ducked just as the door opened and someone looked in. Between the bed legs, Morag saw the silhouette of ape-like feet in the doorway. Kang took a few heavy steps into the room. Then as suddenly as he had arrived, he was gone.

'Is it safe?' Morag whispered to Montgomery.

'Not for long. He'll be back,' he replied. 'Come on, we have to get out of here. Aldiss needs us.'

With her heart beating wildly, Morag picked up the paintings and followed Montgomery to the door. He opened it cautiously and glanced outside. The corridor was empty. They slipped out and sneaked downstairs. Along the corridor they ran towards the secret door, and under the cover of the growing darkness they bolted for the undergrowth beyond the path. They stopped for a few minutes, panting.

'Are you all right?' Montgomery asked Morag.

'Yes,' she replied, gradually getting her breath back.

'Let's go,' he said, then stopped. 'Where are Shona, Bertie and Aldiss?'

'Follow me,' said Morag, pushing through the ferns. 'They're close by. I only hope that we're not too late...'

chapter sixteen

Aldiss was barely moving when they found him. The only sign that he was still clinging on to life was the slight trembling of his whiskers. Morag's eyes filled with tears and she could not talk as she handed Mina's tooth to Shona.

'How do we use it?' she gulped, her voice high-pitched and breaking. 'I don't know what to do.'

'Mmpnhhgigrhmppph!' said a voice from Morag's pocket.

Henry! Morag put down the rolled-up paintings of Nathan and Isabella and pulled him out.

'Place it on Aldiss's chest,' the medallion instructed. 'That's right. Leave it there...watch it doesn't roll off.'

He fell silent.

'Do we say something?' Morag asked. She was unable to tear her eyes away from the tooth or from Aldiss. 'Is there a spell?' she demanded. Without thinking, she shook the medallion hard as she spoke. '*What do we do, Henry?*' she wailed.

'Stop shaking me for starters!' he snapped, glaring up at her. Morag's face was white and her eyes were large and worried.

'I'm sorry,' she said quietly and looked away.

'Not at all. I understand,' the medallion replied.

Then he inhaled deeply.

'Now we wait.'

The dragon, who had nursed Aldiss since he had been struck by the dart, frowned.

'Wait for what?' she asked. 'Surely we can't just leave the tooth there. It's not doing anything. It... it...' She gazed down fondly at the little rat lying on his bed of bracken and a great tear rolled down her cheek and plopped to the ground.

'He's going to die, isn't he?' she sobbed and turned away. Bertie threw his wings around her and hugged her tightly.

'It's all my fault,' the dragon cried. 'I wasn't there to protect him. He saved me in the past and I couldn't do the same for him. Now I'll never see Aldiss again!' Her body heaved and shook as her grief poured out.

Morag ran to her and placed her arms around Shona's wide belly, with Henry still dangling from her fingers. Tears of sorrow flowed from her eyes too as she tried to comfort both Shona and Bertie.

'Aldiss! I'm sorry Aldiss! Whooaaaah-ah-ah-aah-hhh!' bawled the dragon, eyes tightly closed.

As the three of them cried they did not notice the tooth brighten with a warm, white glow. Only Montgomery watched as it spread all over the rat's tiny body, enclosing him in a light that was almost too bright to look at.

'Er...' he said trying to attract their attention, but they were too upset to notice.

The light flickered and danced over Aldiss now.

There were tiny tings, the sort of sounds you'd expect from violin strings snapping. Then the light went out and the tooth returned to its normal cream colour.

'Booo hoo hoo...!' Bertie sobbed. He pulled a large red and white polka dot handkerchief from his bag and blew his beak loudly.

He did not notice that Aldiss's paws were twitching slightly, or that his whiskers and nose were flickering, or that he was yawning and slowly opening one eye.

'He was so lovely.' wailed Morag to her friends.

'You're right there. The loveliest rat ever!' Shona agreed. 'He'd laugh if he heard me saying that. He used to tease me because I was afraid of rats.'

'I can't believe he's gone,' sobbed Bertie.

Aldiss opened his other eye and turned his head to see where all the crying was coming from. He sat up and stretched, letting the tooth slide to the ground. The stretch started in his arms, slunk down into his torso and ended with a very satisfying extension of his tail.

'Who's gone?' he squeaked. 'Who are you talking about?'

Morag stopped sobbing. She let go of Shona and turned around. Then a smile swept over her tear-stained face.

'You're alive!' she cried, running to his side. She knelt down, picked him up and hugged and kissed him. The rat waved his little arms and legs.

'Of course I'm alive. What *else* would I be?'

'Oh come here, rodent!' bellowed Shona and snatched him up into her huge embrace.

Aldiss was squeezed and kissed and hugged until he could stand it no more.

'Put me down!' he squeaked. 'You'll squash me!'

They all laughed as Aldiss hopped to the ground and shook his tail.

'You had us all worried,' Morag grinned. 'You nearly died!'

'Me? Not a chance! Are you sure?'

'Don't you remember the tornado in the castle?' tried Bertie. 'Or being hit by the dart?'

Aldiss shook his whiskers.

'Fortunately Morag found just the thing to revive you,' said Montgomery.

Aldiss listened with growing disbelief and looked up at Morag gratefully.

'Thank you for saving my life,' he said.

'Montgomery helped,' she replied, 'and it was Henry who suggested we get the tooth. Where is it anyway?' She scanned the ground. 'Oh, there it is.' She bent down and picked it up by the chain. Nearby, the rolled-up paintings of Nathan and Isabella lay in the grass. She scooped them up and asked Bertie to keep them in his satchel where they would be safe.

The rat turned to the wizard. 'Montgomery, thank you…' he began.

'It was nothing,' the wizard said quickly.

'No it's not. You saved my life.'

'Aldiss we don't have time for this,' the wizard replied. 'I'm glad you're alive, but we must get back to Marnoch Mor. The town needs me.'

And it was then that Morag remembered about his connection to the Eye of Lornish.

'The Eye!' she gasped. 'I'd forgotten all about it.' She looked at Montgomery, scared to ask. 'How much time do we have left to get you back to the Eye?'

'The last time...' the wizard replied. 'Well you were there, you know about the last time—it was four days before the town began to fall apart. You lot managed to get it back to me just in time. There were a few cracks in some buildings, but nothing that we couldn't put right afterwards with magic.' He sighed. 'I've been away from Marnoch Mor for about two days, so that means we still have about forty-eight hours.'

Morag stared at him. 'This time it was different. It was much worse,' she said as she shook her head.

'I don't understand,' he said.

'There was an earthquake only minutes after you disappeared,' Morag explained.

'It was terrible,' added Bertie. 'Buildings were collapsing all over town. Everyone headed to the Town Hall to get answers from the Queen. That's where something unimaginable happened...'

Montgomery's face paled. 'This is impossible. The Eye should protect the town for longer...Tell me what happened.'

'Queen Flora's dead,' said Shona abruptly. 'She was assassinated by the same thing that tried to kill Aldiss.'

Montgomery was stunned. Tears pricked Morag's eyes as she remembered her fear and the anger of the townspeople. 'But everyone thought it was me!'

'Her Majesty told Morag of a secret escape route and we had to use it,' said Bertie.

'The photo booth?' cut in Montgomery. 'Yes, it is reserved for emergencies.'

'Marnoch Mor is being destroyed as we speak,' Morag said, 'and I don't know if we'll get home in time to stop it.'

Montgomery's face was grave. He rubbed his eyes wearily.

'Well,' he said, 'we'd best get back as quickly as we can.' He looked around him. 'How are we getting off this island?' he asked.

As Bertie opened his beak to speak, he was interrupted by a sneering voice from behind.

'You're not going *anywhere.*' They turned round and saw Mephista standing before them, hands on her hips and a triumphant smile on her lips. Tanktop was at her side, sniggering. 'And I'll have the tooth back, if you don't mind,' she added.

She stepped forward and snatched it from Morag before she could do anything about it.

With a twisted smile, Mephista took a wand from her left sleeve and tapped it thoughtfully on her chin before she spoke again.

'You,' she said pointing to the dragon. 'You will make me a pretty penny at the market. Dragon meat is so rare these days.' She looked at the others. 'I suppose I could make slaves of you, but that would really be too much trouble. No, I'll leave you to Kang. He can decide what to do with you.' To Montgomery, she added: 'I was going to offer you up for ransom, but I heard you say Marnoch Mor is falling to pieces anyway, and the Queen is dead. We need a new kingdom, a better Queen. So, why don't you join me and my father in creating a new Marnoch Mor? With your wisdom and my magic, just imagine what we could accomplish together!'

The wizard furrowed his brow and shook his head. 'I will *never* join you,' he growled.

'Not even to save Marnoch Mor?' she said slyly.

The wizard flinched and did not answer.

'As you wish,' she smirked, 'then you might as well be with your friends when I hand them over to the Girallons. Such a pity, I thought you had more ambition than that, Montgomery.'

She raised her wand and flicked it at them menacingly.

'Let's go. Back to the castle with you,' she said. 'Come along, hurry up, I haven't got all night.'

'Do as she says,' Montgomery instructed.

Shona started to protest, but was silenced by a warning look from the wizard. Morag saw it and was puzzled. *Isn't he even going to fight?* she wondered. *Is he so weakened that he is going to allow Mephista to hand them over to the Girallons?* Aldiss scrambled up on to her shoulder and hugged her neck, his soft fur tickling her skin. She stroked him gently, glad of his company, as she reluctantly followed the dragon.

Aldiss whispered to her as she pushed through the undergrowth. 'Why aren't we trying to escape?'

'I know, it's not like Montgomery to give in like this,' she replied. Then she had a thought. 'Get Bertie to create a distraction,' she whispered. 'Don't ask me to explain. I've got a plan and I need your help. Trust me.'

The rat nodded. Without another word he scampered down her body and leapt on to the path. Soon he caught up with the dodo.

Mephista forced them on towards the castle. It was dark now and their only light came from the dull Moonstone Bertie had pulled from his satchel. He went in front, holding it up in his beak as high as he could. Perhaps this was why he did not see the tree root that tripped him and sent him crashing to the ground. Shona and Morag rushed to him immediately.

'What's going on?' barked Mephista. 'Why have you stopped? Tanktop, go and see them.'

Morag heard the great lolloping strides of the Klapp demon as it hurried towards them, smelt its rank breath as it ran, and turned her head as it pushed her out of the way to get to the front of the small crowd.

'Stand!' Tanktop yelled at the bird.

'I can't move. My leg is broken,' Bertie squawked pitifully. Mephista shoved through to the front and looked down at him.

'Get up, you stupid bird!' she demanded. She raised her wand angrily against the terrified dodo and...that was when it happened. Morag jumped up and snatched the wand out of the startled witch's hand and gave her a shove that sent her flying to the ground. It was a foul-tempered, glaring Mephista who pulled herself out of the mud and rose to her feet.

'*How dare you!*' she hissed, brushing the dead leaves from her dress.

'Stay back!' Morag warned, waving the wand. 'We're far enough out of the woods for this to work.'

'You don't know how to use that,' Mephista sneered. 'Now give it back to me and I'll go a bit easier on you.'

'You're right. I don't know how to use this,' Morag admitted. She didn't take her eyes off Mephista. 'But *he* does.' She handed it to Montgomery.

'No!' screeched Mephista.

Montgomery smiled, pointing the wand at her pocket where he had seen her slip it. 'Hand over the tooth,'

Mephista folded her arms and pursed her lips. She glowered at him defiantly. Montgomery, in no mood to take any nonsense, flicked a small firebolt at her. It glanced off the ground near her feet in a bright shower of multi-coloured sparks. She did not flinch. He sent another, closer. This time she jumped.

'Give it to me, Mephista,' he said and held out his hand.

At first it did not seem like the witch would obey, so Montgomery raised the wand at her once more. With a disgruntled sigh, she slipped her hand into her pocket, pulled out the tooth and threw it at him. Montgomery caught it and passed it to Morag, who put it in the pocket of her dress.

'Well, Mephista, it looks like you are now *our* prisoner, you and the...where's that Klapp demon?' he asked, searching the darkening forest. He sniffed, but no tell-tale dead fish smell could be detected on the wind. 'He's probably headed back to the castle to alert the guards!' he said. He glanced around anxiously at Morag, Bertie, Aldiss and Shona and made a quick decision.

'We need to get off this island fast!' he said, urgently. 'You still haven't told me how we are getting off.'

'Kyle is waiting offshore in the *Sea Kelpie*,' said Morag.

Bertie showed him the small radio the fisherman had given him so he could tell their friend when they were ready to leave.

'I'll call him right now and get him to meet us,' he said. The radio crackled. 'Where will he be able to pick us up? There's no jetty other than the one in front of the castle.'

Montgomery turned to Shona. 'Is there a cove or somewhere out of sight of the castle where Kyle can bring his boat?'

'The island's changed a lot since I grew up here,' she replied. 'But there's a place a few miles from here, back in the direction of Dragon's End.'

'Bertie, let's get him to meet us there,' Montgomery instructed. The dodo nodded and spoke into the radio.

'Now, Mephista,' said Montgomery. 'There's something you must know about your father...' But he got no further. Suddenly he cried out in pain and crumpled to the ground.

'Montgomery?' Morag squealed. She knelt beside him as he contorted in agony. He moaned and his breathing became shallow.

'Aldiss, get me a light!' she cried.

The rat found the Moonstone and brought it over. Morag knelt in the cold earth and held Montgomery's weakening hand. When Aldiss held up the Moonstone he squeaked with shock. Even Mephista gasped. Montgomery's face had suddenly transformed into that of a tired old man, lined and pale. His normally dark and shining hair was white and falling out in clumps.

'What's the matter?' Bertie cried, dropping the radio on the grass and flapping over.

'Something's seriously wrong with Montgomery,' Morag replied, tears welling.

'It's the Eye'. The wizard's voice was thin and strained. 'It's dying. And so am I. I...need...to get home. We need to be...together again.'

Morag looked at the others. The Eye was dying and now Montgomery's life was draining away before their eyes. But he was not the only one in peril. 'Stay with him,' she said. 'I have to go back to the castle.'

'Whatever for?' asked Bertie.

'I promised Chelsea she could come with us. I can't go without her, after all the help she's been.'

'But there's no time!' Bertie protested. 'You'll have to leave her behind.'

'I can't just run away!' the girl sobbed.

'Morag, listen to me,' said Shona shaking her by the shoulders. 'You can either save Chelsea or you can save Montgomery. But there isn't time to save both. Go back to the castle and find Chelsea if you feel you have to. But there will be no home to take her to if Montgomery is dead when you get back. No home for her, you or us. Marnoch Mor will be gone.'

'Who are you going to save, Morag?' asked Aldiss after a pause.

Morag chewed her lip until it bled as she mulled one of the most difficult decisions of her young life.

'Help me get him to his feet,' she said eventually.

***

Although Shona was able to support him, it took Montgomery a great effort to rise from the ground and stand again. The attack had come so swiftly that it had drained all the energy from him. He was shaky, but able to straighten up after a few moments. His expression, in spite of the newly appeared wrinkles, relaxed a little. He managed a smile and nodded when Morag asked him if he was able to walk.

'We need to get away,' he said, 'before the demon gets help.'

On seeing Morag's worried face, he added mysteriously: 'You, of all people, mustn't worry. The pain has gone. I promise...'

chapter seventeen

The band of friends and their prisoner moved slowly through the dark forest, stumbling over large rocks and gnarled tree roots sticking out of the ground. They kept off the path in case they were seen by the Girallons, but stayed close to it so as not to get lost in the wood's eerie blackness. The hunting horn had sounded shortly after their departure from the clearing, and they knew it was only a matter of time before the Girallons appeared.

Aldiss scampered in front, followed by Bertie, who kept Mephista's wand firmly fixed on the flame-haired sorceress, while Shona and Morag held up Montgomery. Morag could feel him wince and twist as spasms of pain shot through his body.

After they had walked for half an hour, Aldiss waved them to a stop where the trees petered out into blackness.

'Wait! I can smell the sea,' he said.

'Is this really where we've to meet Kyle?' Bertie rasped at Shona.

Shona placed a claw firmly around Mephista's waist to stop her from trying to escape, and craned to look around. The witch folded her arms and rolled her eyes. It was dark and it was hard to see anything in front of them.

'I can't be sure if this is the right spot,' the dragon said. 'It feels different.'

A thin, eerie call came from somewhere in the woods behind them. It was closer now than before and when Morag looked back between the trees she saw the tiny flickers of flaming torches a few miles away and felt sure she heard the sharp yelps of hunting dogs, slavering at the scent of their prey.

She looked at Montgomery. His eyes were closed and his lips tightly drawn but he was still breathing.

'It'll have to do,' she said guiding the stricken wizard through the undergrowth in the direction of the cliffs. 'Come on, let's go. We'll find a way down to the shore.'

With the others following, Morag led Montgomery into the thick of the damp undergrowth. Ferns, long grasses and trees sought to stop her, but although she was exhausted and cold, Morag was determined. Ignoring the heaviness of her legs, which were shaking with tiredness, she pushed on through the wet grass until the ground fell away from her and she stumbled onto a high ledge, about ten metres above the sea. In the dull moonlight, she could just see the spiky waves smack against the foot of the cliff, throwing up wild froth and freezing spray.

As the others followed, Morag felt herself being pushed forward and it was all she could do to stop herself from toppling into the icy black waters below. She looked along the cliff side and searched out across the horizon but saw nothing but a dark, troubled sea under a black sky.

'What if something's happened to Kyle?' Morag wondered out loud.

'Now, now, we mustn't worry about him,' hushed Bertie, 'He won't let us down.'

The Girallons' hunting horn cut through the air again, closer this time, keener than before. Although she was still gripped by Shona, Mephista looked as if she had already won. 'If I were you I'd worry about yourselves,' she smirked.

'Look! There he is!' cried Aldiss, pointing.

A little way out, bobbing gently in the water, was the sanctuary of the *Sea Kelpie*.

Morag cried out with joy, but was cut short by Shona. 'He's too far out,' she said. 'There's no way to get to him.'

'Give me Henry and the tooth...' Montgomery gasped.

He was hugging his body tightly and, to Morag's horror, his face now looked even older than it had in the clearing. Deep lines ridged his forehead and encased his eyes. His cheeks were hollow and wrinkles had begun to appear under his chin.

'What are you going to do?' the girl asked, handing over the medallion and the tooth. Henry gleamed in what little moonlight there was and seemed to be smiling, as if he knew what was coming next.

'Watch,' replied the wizard.

Montgomery whispered to Henry, who seemed to nod, although Morag could not work out how. He closed his tiny eyes and started a long low chant which gradually grew in intensity. Some minutes had passed when suddenly the tooth began to glow brightly. Montgomery placed the tooth on the ground and an arc of light blazed across the waves to the boat. Montgomery took a breath before speaking.

'It's a bridge. Who'll be first to walk over it?' he gasped. 'It's quite safe for you all.'

'What about you?' Morag asked. She could sense that he meant to stay behind.

'I'll follow,' he said. 'Someone has to stay with the tooth. Go...please...'

The Girallon horn sounded again—their scent had clearly been picked up—and Morag felt the earth tremor as the burly creatures thundered towards them. She looked back at her friend again.

'*Now*, Morag!' Montgomery hissed.

The girl hesitated no more. As soon as she stepped into the light she was pulled across the ledge, as if on a moving walkway in the human world. There was no sound, only bright light surrounding her. She wasn't even sure if her friends were following, but she trusted Montgomery. Seconds later, she found herself stepping down onto the deck of the fishing boat and looking into the startled face of Kyle.

'Hey! What happened...?' he began.

'I'll tell you later,' she said as Bertie appeared in a flurry of grey feathers behind her. Aldiss leaped down next, followed by a disgruntled Mephista held by Shona. They all stood together on deck, ignoring the piercing cold wind that whipped their hair and feathers around in a frenzy.

'Where's Montgomery?' Morag asked.

'And why is he taking so long...?' continued Bertie.

Seconds turned into a minute, then another, and finally a shape appeared before them. Montgomery materialised, smiled weakly and then collapsed. The tunnel of light immediately blinked out and Morag ran to him.

Mephista made to move until she saw Bertie lift her own wand in warning. She raised her hands and stood still.

'I don't feel so good,' said Montgomery before his eyes closed.

'Help me get him downstairs!' yelled Morag. 'Kyle, get us out of here. Girallons are hunting us and we need to get to Marnoch Mor as soon as possible otherwise Montgomery will...will...'

She couldn't say the word. She couldn't believe that he might die. With Aldiss opening doors for them, Shona helped Morag carry the ailing wizard down below. They laid him on a bunk, where Morag pulled a woollen blanket over him. She smoothed his whitened hair from his forehead.

'He'll be all right, won't he, Shona? Once we get him home? Everything will be fine. Won't it?'

The dragon said nothing, but laid a consoling claw on the little girl's shoulder.

Kyle hauled in the anchor and ran to the wheelhouse. He started the engine and plotted a course heading east towards the mainland.

Once she had dried her eyes, Morag went back up on deck and saw the witch looking back to the DarkIsle, gazing at the torch-illuminated outline of the castle. She did not seem to care that Morag was there, just kept on staring at her home.

'My father will be furious with you,' Mephista sneered. 'He will be hatching a plan to get me back right now. He'll come after us, you know.'

In the darkness, Morag's eyes twitched at the thought of another confrontation and she was glad the witch could not see her discomfort.

'Your father is not who you think he is,' she said at last.

'Don't you dare tell me I don't know my own father,' Mephista said. Through the darkness, Morag sensed the witch was smiling. 'It's only a matter of time before he finds me. And when he does, you'll wish Tanktop had thrown you to the wolves.'

Morag staggered back and walked up to the wheelhouse, where Kyle was pushing the fishing boat to its limits. It was a small and nimble craft that was capable of a fast rate of knots, but it had its limitations. In the brightness of the lone bulb, Morag saw how serious and determined he was. He managed to smile when she joined him at the wheel.

'Any sign of them coming after us?' the fisherman asked, keeping his eyes glued on the dark sea rising and falling in front of them.

'Not so far, but Mephista says it's only a matter of time,' Morag told him. Her throat tightened at the prospect of seeing the resurrected warlock again, of looking into those cold dead eyes.

'What does *she* know?' Kyle smiled. 'I bet that without Her Ladyship everyone in the castle will be celebrating, Morag.'

'*Morag?*' repeated a disembodied girl's voice. Morag looked at Kyle in alarm. '*H-hello Morag? Are you there?*'

Kyle's radio was crackling with static, but they could hear the voice coming through it quite clearly.

'Chelsea? Is that you?' asked Morag.

'*Yours truly. I found a radio in the clearing. It's not like anything we have on Murst, so I guessed one of you guys must have dropped it.*'

'I-I wanted to come back for you, Chelsea, honestly. But Montgomery was too sick for me to leave him.'

'*It's okay. I thought you might have to leave in a hurry. Listen, I can't talk for long. I just had to thank you. There's chaos here! Mephista and Tanktop are missing, and Kang and Devlish and all the Girallons have left the castle. I've freed all*

*the men they took from the village and we're tak-
ing control of the castle. I'm just waiting here for
my gran. She's bringing re-enforcements from
Dragon's End. They're going to have quite a fight
when they come back! It's amazing!'*

Morag wanted to cry and laugh at the same
time. 'You make it sound like fun.'

*'Believe me, it's been a long time since we felt
this free! All thanks to you and the Ancient One.'*

***

As time went on and they got further away, Morag
began to relax a little and even joined her friends
downstairs. Mephista, seemingly unconcerned
by the ice cold sea spray that was drenching her
dress and dampening her normally glossy hair,
stayed at the railings, keeping a vigil for her father. They let her. She was no threat to them now.

'Squid's eye soup anyone?' Bertie said, sticking
his wing into his bag.

Morag shook her head. 'No thank you.'

'A Spruggit sandwich? No?'

'Nothing to eat for me, just tea,' the girl said,
glancing anxiously over to where Montgomery
lay. He had not woken up and she was worried
about him. His face was grey and drawn, his
hair was falling out as she watched, the lines
on his face deepening, his body becoming frail
and gaunt. He moaned slightly and then was still
again.

What are we going to do? Morag fretted to herself. *What if he dies before we can get him home?*

Suddenly her thoughts were interrupted by a loud cackle from above. It was Mephista. Startled, Morag glanced at her friends and scrambled to her feet. Taking the stairs two at a time, she rushed up and into the open. There, Mephista was dancing from foot to foot, her hands punching the air with delight.

'You! I told you he would come! I told you!' she whooped, excitedly pointing in the direction of Murst, her long white fingers stabbing the air as if she were parrying with the night. She turned on Morag. 'Now you'll be sorry!' she hissed.

Morag squinted to see what the witch had been pointing at. The sky was thick with heavy dark clouds, interspersed with little pockets of the deepest black and the odd star. At first Morag could only see the distant outline of the castle silhouetted against the sky, nothing else. No... wait...what was that in the sky? Something large, something blacker than the night. A large ebony gondola, carried through the sky by hundreds of bats, cut through the clouds and hurtled towards them.

Morag ran to the wheelhouse where Kyle was singing quietly to himself. 'It's Devlish!' she cried, and without pausing for breath, 'He's heading this way—fast!'

'That's not good,' Kyle said, 'I've got the *Kelpie* going as fast as she can. She can't go any faster.'

'Is there nothing you can do to make her speed up?' Morag asked, not bothering to keep the desperation from her voice. 'There must be *something.*'

He shook his head. 'I'm not the one who can do magic. I'm just a fisherman! Why don't you ask your friends if they can help?' he asked.

Henry, still clutched in Montgomery's lifeless hand, was the only one to come up with a plan. 'Get me out of here,' he mumbled from behind Montgomery's fingers, 'and bring me the tooth.'

It took Morag and Bertie a few minutes to prize him out of Montgomery's hand. At first, his fingers were too stiff, but after some tugging they managed to open them long enough.

'Now, put me down on the table, place the tooth on top of me and leave me to it,' Henry ordered.

Morag did as she was told, then Henry added: 'Run upstairs and keep an eye out for Devlish. This spell may take a few moments and he mustn't catch up with us before it's worked.'

As Morag climbed the steps the medallion began to utter unintelligible magic words. She opened the door and immediately heard Mephista shouting on deck.

'I'm here father, come and get me!' She jumped up and down and waved.

'Be quiet, woman!' flustered Bertie, holding Mephista's wand in his trembling wing, 'or you'll leave me with no choice but to use this.'

She looked down at the dodo and scoffed. 'You

wouldn't know one end of that wand from the other. You belong in a glass case with all the other extinct beasts.'

'How dare you!' Bertie spluttered in outrage.

'Don't talk to him like that,' cried Aldiss, standing between them with his paws on his hips. 'I'll have you know Bertie is a Trainee Wizard who—'

'And YOU...' Mephista snarled, 'well, I don't need a magic wand to deal with vermin.'

She threw her head back and laughed, but now her voice sounded different, almost muffled. Morag, Aldiss and Bertie were silent as they watched a bubble swell over and around the *Sea Kelpie*.

Mephista shrieked and climbed up on the railing, to pummel the bubble with her fists. The membrane stretched and squeaked, but did not tear.

'What's going on?' Morag asked Henry when she went back to the cabin.

'It's like the shield that covers Marnoch Mor. It should keep us invisible until we get home,' he told her proudly.

'Are you sure about that?'

'Totally. The spell isn't permanent but it should last long enough.'

But Morag was not convinced and went back up to be with Bertie and Aldiss to watch for Devlish's gondola. Once she had found the black dot growing in the sky, gleaming like a dark star, she could not take her eyes off it.

'I'm here!' screamed Mephista.

With her heart in her mouth, Morag watched as it sped towards them out of the night sky. Now she could clearly see the warlock's red hair flickering like flames from the top of his head. His skull-white face, the contemptuous grimace, and his wild staring eyes, sent chills down her spine. Beside him, aiming a crossbow was the four-armed captain of the Girallons, Kang. He was shouting, but from inside the bubble, Morag could only guess at what he was saying.

The cloud of a thousand bats strained at their reins as the warlock forced them to fly faster. Bertie covered his eyes with a wing and Aldiss hid behind Morag's coat. She continued to stare straight ahead but was silently praying that the spell was working.

Mephista shrieked with joy as the dark hull bore down on the *Sea Kelpie*. But it flew over, soaring past them. Morag let out a long sigh of relief. Henry had been right; Devlish had not seen them and was flying on.

'I don't know why you're looking so pleased with yourself,' snapped Mephista. 'My father is not only looking for *me*, he's looking for *you* too. He'll find us and when he does *you'll* be sorry. And no amount of magic will prevent my father—the greatest warlock who ever lived—from finding me. Mark my words.'

The witch stormed past the girl to the cabin door, but suddenly came to a halt. Something in the sky had caught her attention. A smile of triumph lit Mephista's face. Looking up, Morag could see that Devlish's gondola had turned and was rocketing back towards them.

'I told you. He was not fooled by your paltry magic. His is more powerful. He's coming back,' laughed the witch.

'Kyle, change direction! Devlish is headed straight for us!' Morag shouted.

The fisherman waved from the door of the wheelhouse and the boat shifted to the south.

'Morag!' squealed Aldiss. 'Shona! Help, quick!

Spinning round, Morag saw Mephista had snatched Bertie up by his leg and was holding the flapping dodo at arms' length.

'The wand!' cried Shona, bounding out of the wheelhouse. But Mephista had plucked it from Bertie's wing and now held it up above her head.

With a wicked smile, she casually tossed Bertie down the cabin stairs. He crashed to the bottom with a yelp. Squeaking with fright, Aldiss ran to him. Shona clenched her fists and lunged at the witch.

'No closer,' Mephista said coldly. Behind her, the prow of Devlish's gondola was nearly upon them. 'The chase is over I'm afraid,' she smiled. 'And now you belong to me and my father.'

'But that's just it, Mephista,' Morag began. 'That's not Devlish. Something else has taken over his body.'

'Nonsense!' Mephista pointed the wand, growled a low spell and shot a stream of lightning from the tip to the transparent dome above the boat. 'I hate to burst your bubble...' she cackled.

The dome flickered like a candle going out. But a flash of golden sparks on the deck made Morag jump. A ball of fire smashed the wand from Mephista's grasp and cut off the beam of energy. The witch screamed as she fell to her knees. Morag and Shona turned.

A battered dodo stood in the doorway, triumphantly holding up a gold medallion.

'I'm not ready to be put in a glass case just yet, thank you,' Bertie said.

'You idiot bird!' screeched Mephista. 'Don't you see? If you've made this boat invisible again that means my father won't see us and—'

'And that's *too bad!*' Aldiss piped up.

'For you. Because—'

'He'll crash straight into us...' interrupted Shona.

There was a deafening roar and Morag's ears popped as the deck lurched from under her feet, and feathers, fur, scales, and red hair were thrown together in a bone-jarring rush. Morag was slammed against the railings and thought she heard Kyle yell, 'Hold on!' and someone else squawk, 'Lifebelts!' and a third little voice in the terrible dark cry, 'We're going under!' as the *Sea Kelpie* tipped and sank beneath the waves.

chapter eighteen

The next morning, Morag awoke with a splitting headache, slumped against the wall of the wheel-house. As she prised her eyes open, she focused on a fuzzy, but familiar shape. It was bright-eyed and feathery and was smiling in a way that only a dodo could.

'Good morning merry sunshine!' chirped Bertie. 'How are we this morning?'

'Mmmmm?' was all Morag could manage.

'Tea?' the chipper bird offered. He handed her a steaming mug of weak black Earl Grey. The girl took the mug gratefully and held it in her cold fingers for warmth.

'What happened?' Morag asked. 'There was a crash...And we sank...Did I hit my head?' She looked around at the empty room. 'Is Kyle all right?' There was no fisherman in sight.

'He's having a well-earned rest,' said the dodo. 'I'm in charge for now.'

Morag pulled herself up to a proper sitting posi-tion and stretched her back. She moaned slightly as a sharp pain shot down her spine. 'What hap-pened last night?' she asked.

'Devlish's gondola hit us and we turned over. If it hadn't been for the bubble around the boat we would have sunk. Mephista's interference weak-ened the spell and it's worn off now, so we're fully visible again.'

'What's happened to her?'

'Kyle locked her up in his cabin.'

'Why don't I remember any of this?'

'You and she were knocked out. Morag, what did you mean last night when you told her some-thing else had taken over Devlish's body?'

'Montgomery and I overheard Kang talking in the castle. It seems Kang arranged for some kind of horrible creature to take over Devlish's body without Mephista knowing. Something called Amergin...'

'A Mitlock Demon!' gasped the dodo.

'You've heard of him? I tried to get it out of Montgomery, but he wouldn't say.'

'Mitlock Demons are powerful, evil creatures from the dark side. Suddenly Devlish doesn't seem so bad...'

'Hang on, the boat's stopped moving. Where are we, Bertie?' Morag asked.

Bertie looked down at his claws and when she tried to look him in the eye, he became shifty.

'Well?'

The dodo let out a long sigh before replying. 'Irvine,' he said quickly, as if saying it fast would negate its meaning.

'Irvine? What are we doing *here*?' the girl re-plied in a panic. 'I can't be in Irvine, it's too dan-gerous. What if Jermy and Moira see me? What if someone recognises me and tells them I'm here? They'll come and get me and make me be their slave again. Why are we *here* of all places?'

'It was the only coastal place we could land that had a Secret Underground Station,' he explained. 'Kyle said the boat was being pushed south by bad weather and Devlish was still hanging about. He had no choice other than to land here.'

'Surely we could have gone *some*where else,' she said desperately as she glanced out of the windows, eyes frantically searching for her former guardians. 'There are loads of places we could have dropped anchor.'

The dodo shook his head. 'It was impossible I'm afraid.'

'Bertie, they'll find out I'm here and drag me back to their horrible house,' she argued with tears welling in her eyes.

'I'm sure it won't come to that,' said the bird. 'I mean, how could they see you? You're hidden in a boat and we're all here to protect you.'

'Hmmm. Montgomery would have found another way,' she said. Then she remembered. 'Montgomery! How is he? Is he better?'

The dodo looked away. 'He's sleeping, but he's not improving,' he answered. Then he closed his eyes and she knew it was bad news. 'Morag, I don't think Montgomery has long to live.'

'Then we must get him to the Underground now, and take him back to Marnoch Mor so he can be with the Eye again.'

Bertie shook his head solemnly.

'Why not?' she asked.

'It's too dangerous. We might be seen. We'll have to wait for nightfall until we can look for the cave that leads to the Underground.'

'But you said Montgomery hasn't long to live.'

The bird sighed. 'We have no choice. A dodo and a dragon can't risk being seen by humans. And Aldiss has a terrible sense of direction...'

Shona agreed. 'Bertie's right, it's out of the question!' she told Morag when the plan was put to her. A dragon and a dodo can't leave the boat in broad daylight. The moment we step off someone will call the police and have us caught. I'll end up being prodded by scientists and Bertie will become a zoological phenomenon. It'll be foolhardy even to try.'

Morag pursed her lips. '*You* can't risk it, but *I* can. *I'll* take him to the cave by myself,' she decided. 'You lot can take a different route—a longer one if necessary—and keep out of sight. You can join us as quickly as you can.'

'But what about Jermy and Moira?' said the dodo.

Morag considered this for a second, then said, 'I'll just have to risk it. I can't let Montgomery die. I have no choice.'

Aldiss, however, was in favour of Morag's plan. 'She's right, we can't wait until it is dark. Montgomery will have faded away by then. We have to do something now. I'll come with you, Morag.

I won't be as conspicuous as Shona and Bertie.'

Morag looked at her friends and totted up the votes: two in favour, two against. What did Kyle think? And Henry? The medallion was resting on top of the unconscious Montgomery, a worried expression on his tiny face. They had been together for many years and he was terrified that he was about to lose his best friend. Henry immediately agreed with Morag. That left Kyle. The fisherman, exhausted from being up all night at the wheel, just wanted to be left alone in his bunk. He knew about Montgomery's condition, but all he could do was mumble a few words to Morag before he turned over and slipped back into sleep. Morag left him snoring and returned upstairs to the deck.

'What did he say?' Shona and Bertie wanted to know.

'He thought *my* plan was the best,' she decided, 'so I need Bertie to help me get Montgomery up on deck and then Shona can lift him off the boat. I'll take it from there.'

'But—' the dragon began, however her protestations fell on deaf ears, for Morag was too busy working out how she was going to get Montgomery across the dunes.

Kyle had docked the boat in a harbour close to the town of Irvine, which had been Morag's home until Bertie and Aldiss had rescued her from Moira and Jermy's basement. Morag knew the area well. It was nice to be back...well, almost. She glanced around nervously. *I'm just being silly,* she told herself, *there is no way Moira and Jermy can know I'm here.* A cold wind brushed over her face, pinking her cheeks, and tugging at her hair. She brushed it aside with a gloved hand and fumbled with the buttons on her coat. It was cold this morning. She had better make sure Montgomery was well wrapped up.

The wizard had not moved when she went below deck. His face was as grey as the winter sky, his hair nearly white and the lines on his face deeper and more pronounced. He was barely breathing.

'Montgomery?' Morag said softly.

The wizard moaned.

'If you can hear me, I need your help,' she said, pulling on his shoulders. 'I need you to sit up. Please try to sit up for me. I can't do it myself.'

She pulled and she yanked and she heaved, but she could not get him upright. She let go and stood back.

'Bertie, help me,' she said as the bird flapped down the stairs.

He waddled over and did his best, but even two of them could not get him to sit up.

'This is useless,' said Morag, close to tears. 'We'll never get him to the cave in time.' She sat down forlornly.

'Can't Kyle help?' Bertie suggested.

They both glanced over to the corner where Kyle was fast asleep on his bunk. He snored loudly. Morag shook her head.

'Point me to him,' said Henry from Montgomery's chest. 'I think I might be able to magic him up on deck.'

'Henry! Do you really think you could?' said Morag.

'My magic's nearly run out after last night's escape, but I think I might be able to muster some from somewhere.'

He instructed her to prop him up on a table so he could see the wizard. Then he contorted his face into all sorts of shapes and angles, and he grunted and groaned as he tried to find some trace of magic within him. With his eyes closed in concentration, the medallion stopped for a moment and was still. Then...

He burped loudly, opened his eyes, excused himself, and smiled. 'It's done,' he said smugly.

Morag turned round to look, and sure enough Montgomery had disappeared.

'Upstairs,' Henry said by way of an explanation.

Morag rushed up on to the deck. It was cold up there and a light rain had begun to fall. She could see no one except Shona, half-hidden under a tarpaulin. Where was Montgomery? Aldiss waved to her and there, propped up beside him, against the base of the wheelhouse, was the ever weakening wizard.

'Wait here,' she told Aldiss, 'I'll get something to put him in. There's no way we can carry him to the cave on our own.'

'Hurry, Morag!'

While the rat stood guard by the unconscious Montgomery, Morag set off in the direction of a row of houses, and knocked sharply on the door of the first one she came to. An old woman with long straggly hair answered. 'Yes? What can I do for you?' she asked.

'I wonder...' ventured Morag, looking at the woman's tidy garden. 'I wonder if you have a wheelbarrow I could borrow?'

'A wheelbarrow? What does a little girl want to play with a wheelbarrow for?' the woman asked. 'Haven't you got dolls or a skipping rope?'

'I'll only be a few minutes, and I won't take it far, honestly.'

'I have visitors. I can't just leave them to get the wheelbarrow out of the shed. Is it important?'

'I just need to use it to get something down to the beach. It won't take long and I'll come straight back with it.'

'All right, dear, but make sure you return it right away. My John will have a fit if his wheelbarrow goes missing. Come in.'

The woman led her down a small hallway towards a frosted glass door. Through it Morag could see the vague outlines of the lady's visitors, a man and a woman, sitting on the sofa. 'Now, pet, you go into the living room and make yourself comfortable while I go and fetch it.'

'Thank you,' said Morag gratefully as she watched the woman disappear into the kitchen.

When she pushed open the living room door Morag didn't know who was more surprised: her or the people sitting there before her. She felt the colour drain from her face as she realised who they were.

'Jermy! Moira!' she cried.

Jermy immediately sprang to his feet. 'You little brat!' he snarled and lunged to grab her.

Morag jumped, but he was too quick for her. Before she knew it, he had her by the hood of her coat. 'Let me go!' she shouted.

'Well, well, well,' smirked Moira, a cigar dangling from her lips, 'if it isn't our little lost lamb. What will the papers say about this one, my love: we've been searching for her for weeks and here she just waltzes back without a word. What luck! Isn't it lucky, Jermy? Pity we don't have a camera.'

'Yes, my sweet,' he agreed. Morag could feel his hot rancid breath on her cheek and she turned away, disgusted. His teeth were yellow from tobacco stains and a lack of brushing and there was a large poisonous spot on his cheek. He smiled when he saw her looking at him.

'Missed me, have ye?' he asked.

'Definitely not!' the girl replied. 'Let me go. You have no right to keep me here.'

'We have every right, my dear,' replied Moira. She too was still her awful self. Her hair, dyed bright red, stuck up like wire. Her makeup was garish and looked like it had been applied with a trowel. There were stains on her tatty green dress. 'You belong to us. You're our own dear daughter come back to us.'

'I was never your daughter,' snapped Morag, who was not afraid of this pair any more. 'And I never will be!'

'Sorry, pet, but he must have put the wheelbarrow somewhere else,' said the woman opening the door. 'Is something wrong?' She looked puzzled.

'No!' said Moira grinning. 'Things couldn't be better. In fact, a miracle has happened. This here is our own dear missing daughter Morag, come back to us at long last. What do you make of *that*? She must have wandered off and lost her memory. We've missed her terribly around the guesthouse.'

'That we did, my dear,' Jermy simpered.

'Get your hands off me,' growled Morag, kicking and twisting to break free of Jermy's tightening grip. 'These two are *not* my parents. Please help me. Call the police. Do something!'

The shocked woman glanced from Morag to Jermy and Moira and then back to Morag again. She looked unsure of what to do next. Then, to Morag's surprise, she burst out laughing.

'Well, I'm glad you finally got that brat back,' she said, patting Jermy on the shoulder. 'Your house was a tip! No-one wanted to visit you any more.' She smirked at Morag. 'Now, make sure you keep her under lock and key this time, Jermy, my old friend. Don't want her running away again.'

'Don't worry about that, Drea,' Jermy replied, a nasty grin spreading over his face. 'She won't get out of our sight this time. She's far too *precious* to us.'

Morag looked up at him as he said this. Precious? Jermy had never made her feel precious in her whole life. What did he mean by it? She didn't have time to ask, for Jermy was already dragging her towards the door, closely followed by Moira, whose spiked high heels clack-clack-clacked. Morag screamed and yelled for help as Jermy shoved her into the kitchen. He pushed her onto a chair and before she knew it she was being tied to it with a washing line.

'Don't think you'll get away with this,' she hissed before Moira bent down to gag her with a red neckerchief. 'My friends will come looking for me. They'll find me, and when they do...mphhg-ghghh!'

Moira tied the gag behind Morag's head as Jermy knotted the rope.

'That should hold her,' he sneered.

'Do you think we should call *her* now?' Moira said from somewhere behind Morag.

'Yes, do it straight away, my love,' Jermy replied, rubbing his bony hands together in glee. 'She needs to know we've got her. The sooner we tell her, the sooner we get our reward.'

'Won't be long now!' Moira laughed. Morag listened to her footsteps clack down the corridor to the living room. There was a muffled conversation between the two women and then she heard the unmistakable sound of someone speaking on the telephone.

'Hello? Is that...?' Moira said excitedly before she lowered her voice. The rest Morag couldn't hear.

Jermy propped his long lanky body up against a kitchen unit and stared at Morag. He looked very pleased with himself. 'I can't believe you just walked in here,' he gloated. 'After all this time, too. What a thing to happen! Me and Moira had just about given up hope of seeing you again.' He laughed. 'It didn't go down well when you ran away,' he continued, more serious, 'Oh no, they didn't like that. You were supposed to stay with us, you see, until they could work out what to do with you. *She* didn't want anyone to know about you, not with the boy and his wife missing. Said it was for your own safety, but we reckoned she just wanted you out the way.'

Morag had no idea what he was talking about. There was the clack-clack of heels again as Moira came back.

'It's all set,' she simpered from the doorway. 'They're coming to get her tonight.'

'And the money? Did you ask about the money?' he barked.

'Course I did, what do you take me for? A moron? We're getting everything that's owed us,' she said. Morag heard her hands clap. 'We're going to be rich, my love!'

Jermy closed his eyes and inhaled deeply as if he were sniffing up every little last bit of her words. He exhaled. 'Say it to me again, Moira, my dear.'

'We're going to be...RICH!' she cackled.

Morag closed her eyes. She didn't care who they had phoned and what the money was for. All she wanted to do was get Montgomery back to Marnoch Mor. She thought about Aldiss waiting by his side at the harbour, while Montgomery's life ebbed away. She opened her eyes and looked around the kitchen for something that might help her escape. There was nothing on top of the kitchen units and there were no knives in sight that might have cut the rope.

'What're you two going on about in there?' came Drea's voice, filtering through from the living room.

Moira and Jermy immediately shut up.

'Er...nothing!' Moira called. To Jermy, she whispered: 'Let's go back through. We may as well wait in comfort. Leave the brat here. She's going nowhere.'

'Good idea,' replied Jermy, heading towards the door. He gave Morag's chair a swift kick as he passed on his way out, making her jump.

I've got to get out of here, thought Morag, *but how?*

chapter nineteen

Morag's arms were numb from being bound and her legs felt like they were being stabbed by thousands of tiny needles. She wondered what time it was and how long she had been there. Would her friends realise something bad had happened and look for her? Through the small kitchen window she could see into a sparse back garden. There was not a soul in sight. Morag sighed.

In the living room, a television was switched on and Morag accepted that she was in for a long wait.

And she was. Hours passed and the girl drifted into an uncomfortable sleep filled with dreams of being pursued by an unknown foe. In one, she was being chased through Murst Castle, but something was wrong with her legs. It felt as if she were wading through thick mud, the type that clung on and didn't let go. She could hardly move; every muscle in her body strained to keep going forward, yet all the time her pursuer was gaining. She turned round to see who it was and screamed as the red-eyed Devlish bore down. He was shouting something at her, but no sound was coming out of his mouth. Morag awoke with a start and it took her a few seconds to realise where she was and what had happened. The kitchen was in semi-darkness and Morag guessed it was late afternoon. She tried to cry out, but the neckerchief was still firmly lodged in her mouth.

There was the distant murmur of voices in the living room, a door squeaked and footsteps walked down the corridor towards her. Her back was still to the door, but she knew someone was standing behind her.

'Time to get you ready, girl,' Jermy growled. 'Moira! Come and help me!'

Moira trotted into the kitchen, dangling a cigar from her thin fingers. From the corner of her eye, Morag watched her drop it on the floor, and grind it into the tiles.

'Now, I'm going to remove this gag,' she said in Morag's ear, 'and you're not going to scream or call for help because if you do, we're going to kill you. Do you understand?'

Morag nodded. Moira untied the kerchief and removed it. Morag coughed, stuck out her dry tongue and tried to lick her lips to get rid of the horrible taste.

'And when I untie you,' said Jermy, glee in his eyes, 'you've to eat something and clean yourself up. We've got a very important visitor coming and you have to look your best so she knows how kind and generous we've been to you!'

Morag opened her mouth to protest, but thought better of it. She could not imagine why anyone important would want to visit Moira and Jermy. She glared up at them as Jermy untied her.

'Stop with the dirty looks,' Moira laughed, 'you're cracking me up!' She played with a long golden chain that was hanging around her neck under her collar. 'I still can't believe it's really you!' she smirked, pulling on the necklace to reveal a large smooth red stone.

Morag gasped. She had seen one just like it somewhere else. She tried to remember. It was in Mephista's room in Murst Castle. Isabella had been wearing one the same in the painting.

'Where did you get that?' she asked.

Moira looked a bit shifty and put the necklace back under her top. 'What, *this old thing?* Jermy gave it to me for our first anniversary,' she replied a little too quickly.

'Let me see it,' Morag demanded, putting out her hand.

'No, you can't,' Moira said, backing away, 'it's mine.'

Morag shook her head. 'It's not, is it?'

'It belonged to Jermy's own dear departed grandmother.'

'I don't believe you. You've stolen it! ' Morag rose to her feet and took a step towards Moira. Jermy got between them.

'Now just a minute,' he said. 'Moira didn't steal it from *you*. She was just keeping it safe, that's all. Until you'd grown up. Isn't that right Moira?'

'Oh yes, my love, absolutely. I was going to give

it back when you were old enough...'

'What?' Morag's mouth fell open. The necklace belonged to Isabella, but they were talking as if it were hers. 'What do you mean?'

'Well, it was in the basket with you when we got you...' he began.

'From the orphanage?'

Jermy and Moira looked at each other. It was clear they knew something.

'We didn't exactly get you from an orphanage,' Moira said slowly, as if telling the truth would bring some major calamity down on top of them all.

'So where *did* I come from?' Morag wanted to know. 'And if that's *my* necklace, why are *you* wearing it?'

'*She* brought you to us after your parents went missing...' Moira went on.

'Moira, my dear, I don't think we should say any more. Not until *she* gets here,' Jermy warned.

'What difference does it make now?' Moira replied. 'She'll know soon enough.'

She went on: 'This and that tatty old book you always carry about with you were the only things in the basket along with you.'

'So you stole it? You took something that had been left for me?' Morag erupted. She could feel rage rattling through her small body. 'Give it back to me!'

She lunged at Moira, who let out a screech. As Jermy pulled her back, Morag missed hearing the ringing of the doorbell. She was not aware of the visitor's footsteps in the hallway. When she heard a polite cough she spun around. The person standing in the doorway made her jump with fright.

'You! It can't be...' she gasped. 'You're dead!'

Standing before her in fine travelling clothes and a long dark cloak was Queen Flora. She smiled warmly. 'Hello again, Morag,' she said, stepping into the dark kitchen. She waved a silver wand and the lights blinked on. Morag winced at the sudden brightness and shielded her eyes with her arm. She squeezed her eyes shut for a second, then opened one, then the other. Still Queen Flora stood before her.

'You died. I saw you,' Morag said, her voice trembling.

'It would take so much more than a poisoned dart to kill me,' the Queen said smugly. 'I am, after all, the most powerful witch in this country. It took me a few days to recover, but I suppose you could say I'm back.'

Morag stared at her for a few moments before it dawned on her that Queen Flora was just the person she needed.

'You've got to help me,' she said, grasping her hands. 'Montgomery's ill, he's dying. I need to take him back to Marnoch Mor immediately. But I've been taken prisoner by these people and they're going to sell me to someone...I don't know who. But I need to get out of here.'

The Queen laughed lightly and prised her hands from Morag's grip. 'My dear, I know all about it,' she said. '*I'm* the person they contacted, and I also know about Montgomery's impending death. How could I not? Marnoch Mor is crumbling as we speak.'

'You? I don't understand,' replied Morag.

'I don't expect you to. How could you, when I left specific instructions that you were not to know anything of your heritage,' she said sweetly. Seeing that the girl was still puzzled, the Queen went on: 'It was I who handed you over to Jermy and Moira to look after when you were still a baby. I had no choice. The people could not know about you, it was too dangerous.'

She walked over to a window and stared out.

'When my son Nathan disappeared...' she began.

'*Your son* Nathan?' Morag cried. 'I know where he...'

'Don't interrupt, dear,' the Queen snapped. 'When he disappeared, I thought my whole world had crashed down around my ears. My only consolation was that *she* had gone too.'

'She?'

'Isabella, the commoner he married.' Flora brushed a tear from her eye and continued: 'I was against the marriage from the beginning. He was promised to another, someone who would unite our great houses, but he chose to go against our wishes and the wishes of our kingdom to marry *her.* If only he had listened to me, things would never have come this far.'

'Who was he supposed to have married?' Morag asked. She felt even sorrier for her friends in the paintings. No wonder they looked so sad.

'Mephista, of the House of Devlish.'

'What?'

'They had been promised to each other from birth. If he had married Mephista, the troubles between Marnoch Mor and Murst would have ceased and we would be at peace. Now, Montgomery is missing and my kingdom is crashing about my ears and it's all because of Isabella.'

'You can't blame Isabella for what's happened,' Morag cried. 'It's not her fault. If anyone's to blame it's that Mephista that you think so highly of. She kidnapped Montgomery to make me go after him—to make me go to Murst. Mephista needed my blood to resurrect her father. That's the type of person she is,' ranted the girl. 'And as for the House of Devlish, didn't you know *they* took Nathan and Isabella?' she demanded.

The Queen's sharp intake of breath proved that she did not.

'How? I would have known if they were holding him prisoner,' she insisted. 'My powers would have found him if he was locked up in a dungeon.'

'But would your powers have found him locked up in a painting?' the girl went on. 'He and Isabella were trapped in paintings in Mephista's room. I've seen them with my own eyes. That's how Devlish hid them from you.'

'Are you sure it is Nathan? I must go to Murst!' the Queen shrieked, face full of concern for her son.

Morag stepped back and looked with disdain at the witch before her.

'Isabella's trapped too,' she said quietly.

'I don't care about that little common witch,' spat the Queen, 'but I *do* care for my son, my heir. Where is he?'

'Safe,' Morag replied. 'They're not on Murst any more. I brought them back.'

The Queen looked overcome.

And then Morag added: 'But before I tell you where they are, you can tell me something. How does this involve me? If you were the one who left me with Jermy and Moira, where did you find me?'

The Queen let out a loud sigh, pursed her lips and looked like she should speak no more.

'Well?'

'My son's marriage produced a child, a girl child. I couldn't let the people of Marnoch Mor know that this foolish marriage had created an heir. I hoped to annul it and make Nathan marry Mephista. So I took the child and hid her. Nathan and his wife went looking for her, but they never came back,' she said, face twisted with spite.

'That's an awful thing to have done,' Morag replied, 'but I still don't understand how this involves me.'

'*You* are their child, Morag,' the Queen said. 'I didn't realise it when you first came to Marnoch Mor. Although you were human, I knew you could be trusted because you'd saved the Eye of Lornish. I didn't find out who you were until a few days ago when the Stokers let me know you were missing. When they told me your full name, the name you were hidden with, Morag MacTavish...well, you can imagine how I felt. By the time I could do something about you, Marnoch Mor was crumbling and you had left to rescue Montgomery.'

'So...if I'm Nathan's daughter,' Morag began, 'that must mean that you are my...'

'Grandmother,' Queen Flora finished.

'How could you?' Morag cried. 'How could you have taken me away from my parents? What kind of a person are you?'

Flora opened her mouth to say something else when there was a violent crash behind them. Everyone spun around to look in the direction of the front door. They heard the sounds of feathers flapping, thumping footsteps and high-pitched squeaks.

'Morag? Where are you? We know you're in here. Aldiss sniffed you out!' squawked a familiar voice.

'Bertie! In the kitchen! Come quickly!' Morag shouted.

'Oh no you don't,' snarled Jermy, grabbing

her by the arms before she could run. 'We were promised money to get you back and we're going to get what's owed us.'

Morag struggled against him, but could not loosen his grip.

'You're going nowhere,' Moira sneered in her ear.

***

Queen Flora clenched her fists and vanished as the kitchen door burst open and a large green dragon filled the doorway, yellow eyes blazing and nostrils smoking with fury. Moira screamed and Jermy gaped in horror.

'Put. Her. Down,' Shona growled very slowly. Jermy snorted. 'I SAID, PUT HER DOWN!' bellowed the dragon.

Face white with fear, Jermy dropped Morag and cowered in the arms of his terrified wife. Shona gave a disgusted snort and blew them a thick cloud of soot that blackened their faces and clothes. Now free, Morag ran to a relieved Bertie and Aldiss waiting in the hallway. Shona snarled a final warning, turned about and ran after her.

'Sorry we took so long,' said the dodo apologetically. 'Aldiss got us lost. Again!'

'It's my nose. I think I'm getting a cold or something,' the rat explained as they bounded down the hallway, over the wreckage of the front door and out of the house.

'Where's Montgomery?' said Morag.

'With Kyle on the boat,' Shona answered. 'He's getting worse. Let's go get him and take him back to Marnoch Mor before anything else happens tonight.'

Morag, who was not sure how to tell her friends what she had learned from the Queen, merely nodded and hurried after them towards the harbour.

'I thought I saw the ghost of Queen Flora back there!' Aldiss laughed nervously, a tiny rat thumb crooked in the direction of the house.

'Yes. It *was* Queen Flora,' replied Morag.

'But she's dead,' said Bertie.

'Apparently not,' replied the girl. 'But that's not the only unbelievable thing that's happened.'

'What do you mean, Morag?' asked Shona.

'I'll tell you all about it on the way to the *Sea Kelpie.*'

***

Back in the kitchen, Jermy turned on the Queen as soon as she reappeared.

'Couldn't you have made that brat invisible as well?'

'Whatever for?' replied the Queen.

'It would have stopped that lot carrying her off,' said Moira.

'But I had to let them rescue her. Morag is going to take Montgomery back to Marnoch Mor,' replied the Queen with a small smile. 'I need her to do that so I can rebuild my kingdom. There will be another chance to stop her, I can assure you of that.'

chapter twenty

'He's dying.'

The words rang in Morag's head as she raced to Montgomery's side. He was lying on the *Sea Kelpie*'s deck, wrapped in a blanket. Only his head showed, but it was enough for her to feel a knot of fear form in her stomach. They didn't have much time. Kyle, who was supporting the dying wizard, gave her a nod when she approached.

'Glad to have you back, Morag,' he said. Shona boarded and lifted Montgomery on to her shoulder, then with a determined intake of breath leaped ashore.

'Safe journey!' the fisherman shouted after them as the friends ran off into the night. 'And good luck!'

Morag, Bertie, Aldiss and Shona with Montgomery over her shoulder, hurried off the harbour road and across the dark grasslands. They ducked at the sight of car headlights and ran when the coast was clear. Morag and Aldiss waded through the reeds and nettles and tall stiff grass until the soil became gritty. Before they could cry out in surprise, they fell off the edge of a dune and tumbled down a sandy slope to the beach. A flapping of wings followed by wheezing and stamping meant that Bertie and Shona were with them.

As they stumbled along the sand, Morag wondered about Mephista, locked up in the *Sea Kelpie*.

'Are you *sure* she won't escape?' she asked.

'Yes, Kyle's checked all the portholes,' replied Bertie matter-of-factly. 'And he's got her wand, so she can't use that.'

'It's only temporary anyway,' wheezed Shona. 'Once we get back to Marnoch Mor, I'll come back with some of the Volunteers and arrest her.'

The wind blew stronger, sending up spray from the incoming tide. Morag looked up at the dark sky and in the chalky moonlight could see the swell of heavy rain clouds sweeping in fast.

'We'd best hurry,' she said, 'I think it's going to pour.'

They stayed on the hard wet sand: it was easier to cross and not so full of broken shells and sharp spikes of driftwood. As they ran, Morag suddenly thought how peculiar they all must look scuttling along the sea shore like this. If anyone saw them, what would they think? It was almost amusing. In her anxiety, Morag almost laughed out loud, but checked herself just in time.

'Are you all right?' Aldiss asked.

She wondered if, in the darkness, the little rat sensed her feelings.

'Yes, fine thanks,' she replied. 'I think...'

'There it is!' shouted Shona. 'Up ahead, follow me!'

Morag tried to see, but in the pale moonlight she found it difficult even to keep track of the dragon. 'Where are you?' she shouted. 'I can't see you.'

'Up here,' called the dragon. 'Climb up, there's a path.'

Morag, Bertie and Aldiss scrambled up the slope, grabbing knots of dune grass to stop them sliding back down. They stumbled and tripped and fell and pulled themselves to their feet until at last they stood on top of the dune. Morag shivered in the darkness.

'Do you think we could have some light here, Shona?' she asked the big black shadow that she hoped was her friend.

'I don't see why not,' Shona replied, her voice low and deep. 'We're far enough down the beach not to be seen by humans. Ask Bertie.'

The dodo fished Moonstones out of his satchel and passed them round. They glowed blue, but were bright enough to see by and soon they found a path that snaked off towards the rocks.

'Never thought I'd be back here,' Bertie grumbled. 'I didn't like it then and I don't like it now. I hate sand. It gets between my feathers and under my beak.'

'Oh stop moaning, Bertie,' Aldiss sighed. 'Oh look! We've arrived.'

Further down the path was the dark opening of the cave that led to the secret Underground Station. Morag looked at it with a small sense of pleasure, for it was here a couple of months before that her life had changed forever when Bertie and Aldiss had agreed to take her to find the Eye of Lornish.

'Shona, put Montgomery inside, out of this wind,' Bertie instructed.

The dragon heaved Montgomery off her shoulder and laid him on a dry patch of earth inside the cave.

'Ooh, is that rain I feel?' the bird squawked, putting a wing up to the skies. 'Everyone else inside too, please!'

Morag and Aldiss rushed in just as the heavens opened and the rain hammered down. Morag held her Moonstone up and scanned the walls of the cave. 'Are you sure this is the right one?' said Morag. 'I can't see the door to the platforms down below.'

She turned to Bertie who had found it last time. The bird shrugged.

'Aldiss?'

'Hmmm,' said the rat, stroking his whiskers thoughtfully. 'Now where were you standing, Bertie, before you leaned against the door and fell down all those stairs?'

'Oh, don't remind me,' winced the bird.

'You bounced all the way down!'

Morag felt along the ragged walls, searching for anything that looked as if it could be a door handle. Halfway between the floor and the wall she suddenly became aware of a knot of stone jutting outwards. She pushed it and the sound of stone grinding against stone filled the cavern until a passageway appeared before them.

'Come on,' she said, stepping inside, 'and Bertie, watch the stairs this time!'

'You don't have to worry about me in that respect!' replied the bird, following her.

It took them only a few minutes to reach the platform at the bottom of the stairwell. The last time they had been there the station had been brightly lit and well looked after. Now the place felt abandoned; the floor tiles were broken and the walls were streaked with water, the bench was tipped over and the Full Moonstones on the ceiling, normally so bright, were flickering dimly. Morag stared at the scene in despair.

'It looks as if it has been closed down. What's happened?'

'I suppose the Eye's influence extended to the Underground too,' said Bertie miserably as the friends gathered on the platform.

'But catching a train was our only hope,' said Aldiss.

'How will we get Montgomery home now?' added Morag.

'Are you folks trying to get back to Marnoch Mor?' asked a voice behind them.

They spun round to see a man with green skin dressed in a train driver's uniform. He had come from one of the tunnels. Morag didn't have time to ask what kind of creature he was but noticed his badge saying *Marnoch Mor Express.*

'Yes, we are,' Bertie replied excitedly. 'Can you tell us when the next train will come?'

'Who knows?' the man replied with a shrug. 'The magic's off for the foreseeable future and the whole Magical Underground Railway network is down. The trains aren't running. Most of them have stopped in the middle of tunnels. The Express I was driving is about half a mile down the track, that way,' he said, pointing.

They all peered, and although they could see no train, several dishevelled passengers were emerging from the tunnel. Three witches carrying new brooms wrapped in brown paper came out first, followed by a couple of gnomes in red hats, three horses, and a pair of ghostly women with floating white hair.

'This way please, magic folk!' shouted the driver. 'We've terminated at Irvine. Remember, it is a human settlement, so please bear that in mind when proceeding with your journeys.'

They grumbled as they climbed the steps to the cave above and when the last one had left, Morag had an idea. She stopped the driver from following the others by grabbing his arm.

'Could I ask you something before you go?' she said politely. He looked at her expectantly. 'Does the train run only on magic produced at Marnoch Mor.'

'I'm not sure,' he replied, scratching his chin, causing little leaves to fall from his cuff. 'I've never tried anything else. Why do you ask?'

'I just wondered if another source of magic could get the train going again, that's all,' she answered.

'Maybe,' he said. 'But I'm not going to try it! Is that all?'

Morag nodded and the driver turned and hurried up the stairs.

'What were you getting at there?' Shona asked Morag.

'I think I may have a solution to our problem,' replied the girl, her eyes shining with hope. 'Come on, let's go and find that train.'

The Marnoch Mor Express was exactly where the driver had said. The door to the last of its three carriages was wide open. They all clambered in, happy to be out of the dark, echoing tunnel. Using the connecting doors, Morag led the band of friends from carriage to carriage until she reached the doorway to the driver's cab. She opened it and smiled.

'Please can you pass me Henry?' she asked, pulling Mina's tooth from her pocket.

Shona removed the medallion from around Montgomery's neck and passed it to her. Then she carried the wizard to a huge pink seat and carefully laid him down.

Henry looked annoyed at being disturbed; he had been enjoying a little nap in the warmth of Montgomery's jumper. 'What now?' he asked.

'I need your magic again,' said Morag, putting

him with the tooth and holding them up. 'Can you make this thing go?'

Henry's tiny eyes swivelled around as he looked at the train's controls. 'I can try,' he said, 'but I can't drive the thing, one of you will have to do that.'

'No problem,' said Bertie, producing another jar of Instant Driver from his satchel and handing it to Morag.

'Let's do it,' said Morag.

'How degrading,' sighed Henry as he got himself ready. 'I am a magical medallion of the highest order, not a bloomin' train driver.'

'Oh, stop whining and get on with it,' Morag hissed.

The medallion threw her a dirty look, closed his eyes and concentrated. Channelling the power of the witch's tooth, Henry mustered all his energies into getting the train moving again. As he did this, Bertie took a glass of water from his satchel, dripped it on the dust from the Instant Driver jar and again a grey train driver materialized.

'We'll be moving in just a moment,' Bertie told him.

'Nothing's happening,' whispered Aldiss.

'Shhhh!' warned Morag.

They waited, but the medallion seemed unable to muster enough magic to get the train started.

'Um...Morag!' Shona called from the carriage. 'I think you should see this.'

'I can't, Shona,' the girl cried, keeping her eyes fixed on Henry.

'Morag, come here now!' the dragon shouted.

Morag looked round with a frown. 'What's the matter?' she called. She put Henry on the dashboard and ran through. The dragon was pointing at the other carriages behind theirs.

'We have company,' she said.

Morag peered through the window in the door at the end of the carriage. Something was moving further down the train. A group were stalking up the aisles towards them. She could see the unmistakeable form of Devlish with his shock of red hair, the four-armed Kang and Mephista.

'How did *she* escape?' the girl gasped in disbelief. 'And how did they find us so quickly?'

'I think your answer is hanging in the air,' the dragon said.

Morag sniffed. A terrible, choking stench was filtering down the train. There, behind the witch, was a scraggy, stinking Klapp demon.

'Tanktop,' spat Morag.

'How did he...? I don't understand,' said Aldiss.

'He must have followed us. They are very good trackers,' said Shona. 'Maybe *he* freed Mephista.'

'Oh no! Do you think Kyle is all right?' cried Morag. 'And we'll have to hide Bertie's bag. It's the only way to save my parents.'

'I'm sure...what? Your parents?' Shona began, then shook her great green head.

'Never mind, I'll explain it all later,' she replied,

returning to the cab. 'Henry, get a move on, they're coming for us.'

Shona bounded down the aisle. 'Hurry!' she shouted to Morag. 'Come and help me uncouple the carriage. It's the only way to stop them getting in here.'

As Morag raced over, Henry concentrated even harder on jolting the train into motion.

'Keep going!' cried Aldiss, shaking his little paws in panic.

'This is most worrying,' said Bertie. 'Maybe *everything* is running out of magic. Maybe there's no magic left...'

Shona wrenched open the carriage door and looked at the coupling: two great iron hooks locked together with bolts.

'No way,' said Morag. 'We need tools to do this!'

Just then the carriage buckled and swayed. Morag looked up. Kang and Tanktop were bounding towards them with bloodthirsty grins.

'Stand back,' said Shona. 'I'm going to smash these things apart.'

'Hurry,' said Morag, voice trembling. Mephista, Devlish, Kang and Tanktop were halfway down the carriage.

'I'm going as fast as I can!' snapped the dragon, tugging and pulling.

'Oh no, Mephista's got her wand back!' Morag gasped, watching as the witch raised it, ready to strike.

'Bertie, Aldiss! They're coming!' Morag screamed.

In the driver's cab, Aldiss was dancing with fear, Bertie was starting to moult and Henry vibrated with strain.

'Henry, we need to go NOW!'

The clang of tearing metal made them jump as Shona fell backwards into the carriage.

'Got it!' she panted, slamming the door behind her, just as a bolt from Mephista's wand struck. The fierce sparks exploded against the window, showering them with fragments of glass. Shona fell, face first to the floor and Morag dived behind the seats as the carriage rocked violently.

'Get up and run!' commanded Shona, crouching against the door. 'They're trying to break through. I can hold them back, but not for long.'

An explosion echoed down the tunnel. There was a deafening screech of metal striking metal. The floor of the carriage shuddered and tilted. Shona watched as Morag staggered to her feet on the unsteady floor.

'Are you all right?' the girl called over.

'Morag—MOVE!'

But instead of running to the driver's cab, the girl threw herself at the dragon. 'You can let go of the door now,' she cried.

'What? But they're right behind us!' said Shona. 'Wait a minute. Are we...? We're moving...'

Morag and Shona peeked out. Behind them the other carriages were fading out of sight. A furious Mephista stood in the doorway of the abandoned carriage, waving her fist as their train sped off.

A loud crack was followed by a rumbling, and they saw the ceiling of the tunnel collapse behind them, obscuring the witch from view. The girl and the dragon looked at each other, shocked. Then, for the first time in days, Morag burst out laughing.

'You were great!' she enthused, leaning in to kiss the dragon. Shona rubbed her jaw.

'You're not hurt are you?' asked Morag.

'No, I broke a tooth when I fell, but I'll live. Are you okay?'

'I'm okay as long as my friends are,' Morag said, hugging her.

chapter twenty-one

Deep underground, in the cool darkness, the little train and its carriage travelled north.

'What are you looking at?' Morag asked Bertie, who was staring at a grid map. The dodo had plucked a train driver's hat from his satchel and it was sitting at a jaunty angle on his head.

'It's a map of the Underground,' the dodo explained. 'I found it under the driver's seat. I thought we could try and bypass Central Station. It would mean we could keep going and not have to change trains. I'm not sure Henry could get another vehicle going.'

They all looked at the medallion lying on the dashboard. His golden face was still screwed up in concentration. On top of him sat the glowing tooth of the dead witch Mina MacPhail.

'We've not found an alternative yet,' he said, breathless with worry.

'What's that?' Morag asked, pointing to a faint trail on the map. It seemed to go underneath Central Station and out the other side.

'We think it's a maintenance tunnel,' explained Aldiss, squeaking with excitement.

'Can't we go through that?'

'We don't know yet,' replied the rat.

They looked at Bertie, who was shaking his head. 'We mustn't take any chances. Let's do it properly and stop and change trains.'

'Why, Bertie?' complained Morag. 'We're already on a train and we all want to go home.'

'We could at least try,' said Aldiss.

'No, it's too dangerous. We don't know what's along there,' Bertie said.

'But if we stop we will waste more time,' the girl said. 'We should keep going, for Montgomery's sake.'

They turned as one and looked into the carriage. The wizard, now looking ancient and white-haired, was lying pale as a ghost across the seats. His face, so lined and grey, was twisted with pain and his breathing was shallower than ever. Bertie gulped.

'We can't risk moving him,' said Shona, who was sitting across the aisle.

'All right, let's do it,' Bertie said.

Stopping temporarily to change tracks, the friends pushed the engine on through the maintenance tunnel. So far underground, the unused tunnel was even darker and spookier and Morag clung to Shona as the little train continued on its journey. Aldiss joined them. He was convinced the tunnel was haunted, having seen tiny lights flutter around and about its walls.

'They're just Tunnel Elves,' Bertie explained with a chuckle, but his frightened rodent friend could not be coaxed back into the cab. 'Get comfortable, we've got a few hours to go.'

Morag rested her head on Shona's great stomach, and cuddled down. There was nothing more they could do except try and get some rest. She closed her eyes and drifted off into sleep.

She dreamt she was back at Murst Castle again, on the seashore next to the wooden jetty. It was a warm sunny day and standing at the end of the jetty was the dead maid. The girl smiled and waved goodbye to Morag, then disappeared before her eyes. Morag sighed and turned over, content she would never be bothered by the maid again, but a new dream formed, something more nightmarish. The white face of Devlish was swimming before her eyes. He was trying to tell her something, but she could not hear him. He shouted and he screamed and he tore at his crimson hair, but still she couldn't tell what he was trying to say. At last he gave up and rushed to seize her. Heart beating rapidly, panting for breath, Morag woke up with a jump and looked around. She was relieved to find herself still on the train with no sign of the warlock.

'Are you all right?' the sleepy dragon asked. Shona yawned.

'I'm fine,' the girl reassured her, 'just had a bad dream that's all. Where are we? Have we arrived yet?'

'I don't know,' Shona replied, scanning the dark windows.

The train had come to a stop in a tunnel and

raised voices reached them from the driver's cab: Aldiss and Bertie were arguing. Morag stood, checked on Montgomery and then joined them. Before she could ask what the problem was, she saw, standing before them on the tracks, Queen Flora accompanied by menacing guards, their pikes held high. Behind them, enticingly close, they could see the tunnel opening into Marnoch Mor Station.

'How did she get back...?' Morag started to wonder, but dismissed the thought. Queen Flora was one of the most influential and talented witches in the magical world. Still, it had been an amazing feat to beat them here.

'What are we going to do?' Aldiss squeaked.

'The only thing we can do,' Morag said. 'I'll go and talk to her. It worked with Ivy.'

The others were dubious, but didn't stop her.

Morag opened the driver's door and climbed down to the track. Straightening her clothes and brushing her hair back from her face, she walked in front of the train. Despite her nervousness, she held her head high and stared straight at Flora as she made her way across the tracks. The Queen did not take her eyes from the girl. She stood there, immobile, and waited until Morag was before her.

'I shall not let you pass,' she said, her soft voice ringing out clearly in the semi-darkness. 'I have reason to believe you mean to bring a contaminant into Marnoch Mor.'

'What are you talking about?' Morag snapped. 'Let us enter. We have Montgomery on board. He needs help.'

'Hand over the tooth and you may enter,' the Queen replied sharply, holding out a white hand. Morag was suspicious. Why did Flora want the tooth?

'I don't have it,' she said. 'Now let us in.'

Flora's eyes flashed angrily and she pursed her lips.

'You lie, little girl,' she growled. 'Give me the tooth and I *may* let you pass,' she added with a hiss.

Morag glared back at her.

'Why do you want it so badly?' she asked. 'It's brought nothing but trouble.'

'I-I want to destroy it! For the safety of all Marnoch Morians,' replied the Queen haughtily. Morag watched her intently. She didn't trust her, but she could see no alternative. Montgomery needed help urgently.

'In that case,' she said, 'I'll go and get it.'

The Queen smiled as the girl ran back to the train and climbed aboard. She watched as Morag spoke with the dodo and the rat, before climbing back down from the cab and walking back towards her. Morag grimaced as she handed Flora the tooth. She didn't know what she wanted it for, but she was sure it was not to destroy it.

Queen Flora's face lit up with joy as she held Mina MacPhail's tooth aloft. She stared at it in wonder and laughed out loud.

'Now I can be truly powerful,' she cried, 'and rule Marnoch Mor as I wish!'

Morag hurried back to the train and instructed her friends to disembark. Shona helped Montgomery to stand and carried him off; still frail, he looked around, bewildered. As Bertie and Aldiss jumped off, Morag grabbed Henry from the dashboard and placed him round her neck. She joined the others on the track and together they made to make their way forward.

'Just a minute,' snarled the Queen. 'Where do you think you're going?'

'We're taking Montgomery home,' replied Morag.

'No, you're not,' Flora said to her. 'Guards, arrest them!'

The sergeant stepped to attention, saluted and ran forward, then halted, puzzled.

'What's the matter?' screamed the Queen. 'Why have you stopped?'

The guard pointed. The Queen's mouth went into an 'O' shape. Morag turned to see what she was looking at. Montgomery, still held in Shona's arms, was bathed in a pure, white, pulsating light. It emitted a buzzing, which grew louder as the brightness increased. Montgomery's long white hair started to shrink and darken, the deep lines in his face smoothed away and he straightened up until he was standing without Shona's support. As they watched, the wizard inhaled deeply and smiled. Then, as suddenly as it began, the light and the buzzing stopped and the Montgomery they knew and loved was standing before them once again.

'That's better,' he said. 'It's good to be so close to the Eye—to feel its energy again.'

'Oh no you don't!' shouted the Queen, holding up the tooth. She began to recite a spell in a low, ominous voice.

Everyone held their breath. But nothing happened.

The Queen tried again. Still nothing. She shook the tooth furiously, but without effect. With a screech, she threw it at them and ran back up the tunnel towards the station.

'Guards—go after her!' Montgomery instructed. 'And place her under arrest.'

The men, momentarily confused, snapped to attention and pursued the Queen. They caught her as she was trying to climb on to the platform.

'What happened to the tooth?' asked Montgomery, retrieving it from the tracks. 'It was one of our most powerful magical artefacts. Has it lost all its power?'

Morag smiled. 'Nothing's happened to it,' she answered. 'That's not Mina's tooth, it's Shona's. She broke it on the train.' She pulled something from her pocket that shone eerily white in the darkness. '*This* is Mina's tooth.' She handed it to the wizard.

'Good thinking,' he said, then sighed. 'Come on, let's get back to the town. We've got a lot of work to do.'

Marnoch Mor Station was still as they had left it after the crowd had smashed their way in. The big wooden doors, their glass panels broken, lay to one side of the entrance. Morag, Montgomery and the others stepped over them as they made their way to the devastation outside.

The sun was just rising as they stood looking at the town square. The rabble from the other night had dispersed, but there were a few stragglers sleeping rough on the ground. They looked up blearily as the friends made their way past.

Montgomery's eyes filled with tears as he saw the broken buildings and torn-up streets of his beloved home. He said nothing as he wandered about, surveying the damage the earthquake had caused.

'Do we know if anyone was hurt?' he asked Bertie.

The dodo shrugged. 'We had to leave before we could find out,' he replied.

Montgomery nodded.

'Very well,' he said, putting his arms out to make a space for himself. 'Stand back.'

As the friends watched, the wizard closed his eyes and frowned in concentration. The glow and the buzzing they had witnessed earlier returned, surrounding him in a bright welcoming light.

Morag looked up to the top of the Town Hall. With Montgomery's return the Eye of Lornish was restored, just as he had been restored by his proximity to it. The stone appeared to be throbbing and sent waves of light breaking across the town. An explosion of sound followed: and immense creaking and whirring as stone collided with stone. A particularly loud bang made them jump. Morag looked at her friends, who were all stunned into silence. *What's happening?* she fretted.

A large rift in the road nearby began to open even further, exposing a dark crevasse below. The friends were preparing to run when suddenly the sides snapped back together and to their amazement, the road appeared to heal itself.

'You've put everything back together,' Morag said breathlessly, and they watched as Marnoch Mor was slowly rebuilt. Morag felt her heart would burst with joy as she witnessed this amazing transformation. She was so proud of Montgomery.

When he had finished, the wizard opened his eyes and smiled. 'That's better,' he said, surveying his work with satisfaction. 'Who's for something to eat? I'm famished. Let's go to the Town Hall and see if they can rustle up something.'

'Great idea,' said the rat, racing off towards its stone steps.

'Don't have to tell *me* twice,' joked the dodo.

'I wonder if they have any pickle...' the dragon mused as she followed.

Only Morag hesitated.

Montgomery frowned. 'Morag? What's the matter?' he asked.

'Well,' she began, 'I don't know where to begin. When I was captured in Irvine, Queen Flora told me something that I just can't believe is true.'

'Come inside and tell me all about it,' the wizard said, putting his arm around her slim shoulders. 'Tales are always better told over a nice cup of tea.'

***

The Town Hall's janitor was more than happy to whip up some tea and scones for the tired friends. They sat in a study that was used by Montgomery when the WWWC met. The sofas were squishy, the fire warming and the soothing lighting made it very hard to stay awake. Morag felt herself growing drowsy. Her eyes closed, but she was still aware of what was going on around her.

'Well, my friend,' she heard Bertie say to Aldiss, 'I think it's about time we retired to our respective homes. I don't know about you, but I'm exhausted.'

'Sounds like a good idea to me,' replied the rat.

There was a scuffling as Aldiss scampered down from the sofa.

'Don't forget your satchel,' he said to his friend.

'Oh! Silly me!' exclaimed the bird. 'Wait a minute, what's this? Morag's paintings! What on earth did she want these old things for?'

At the sound of the word 'paintings', Morag

jolted awake. In all the excitement of the day, she had forgotten about them.

'Give them to me!' she snapped, hand out-stretched for those precious bundles.

Bertie looked at her, startled by her brusque manner, but handed over the paintings without a word. Morag carefully unrolled them and spread them out on the floor. Isabella and Nathan's faces beamed at her.

'Sorry,' she said, 'I should have unwrapped you before now. I was tired...'

'You don't have to explain yourself, child,' said Isabella kindly. 'We're just glad to be away from that dreadful place. Thank you for rescuing us.'

Morag stared at them, a lump rising in her throat. She was so overcome with emotion, she could not talk. It was Montgomery who noticed her strange reaction to the oil paintings.

'Morag,' he said, 'perhaps now would be a good time for you to tell us why these paintings are so important.'

Eyes starry with tears, Morag turned to the wizard. 'Montgomery I'd like to introduce Isabella and Nathan,' she said. 'They were trapped in these paintings by Mephista.'

There was a pause whilst she thought about how she was going to say the next bit.

'They're also my parents.'

There were gasps all round. Shona covered her mouth with a claw, Bertie clasped his chest, Aldiss stared bug-eyed at the girl and Henry looked smug as if he'd known all along. Montgomery looked the most shocked of all.

'You mean you...you're the missing princess?' he stuttered.

'Yes,' replied the girl. 'It seems so.'

'How can that be?' Shona wanted to know. 'You're human.'

And then everyone started talking at once until Morag's head began to hurt.

'Stop!' she cried. 'I want to hear what my mum and dad have to say.'

All eyes turned to Nathan and Isabella.

'I should have known,' said her father, 'you're as beautiful as your mother. You have her eyes. Why hadn't I noticed that before?'

'Are they saying something to her?' Aldiss whispered to Bertie. The dodo shrugged an 'I don't know' to the rat.

'Oh Morag, I'm so glad we have you back,' said her mother. 'When we lost you it felt like our whole world had crumbled. We searched for you...we looked everywhere.'

'I know, Queen Flora told me,' said Morag. 'It was she who took me in the first place.'

'What?' Nathan gasped. 'My mother caused all this?'

'Yes,' replied his daughter, 'but let's not talk about that just now. I'm just so happy to have you both back. I knew you hadn't abandoned me, I just knew it! And I promise I will do everything I can to find a way of releasing you so that we can be a proper family again.'

'How are you going to do that?' Nathan asked.

'I don't know,' she said, 'but I'm sure my friends will help me.'

She looked around to Bertie, Aldiss, Shona and Montgomery who was holding Henry. Although they had only heard one side of the conversation, they had got the gist of it and were all nodding in agreement. Morag smiled. She had a real home at last!

the end

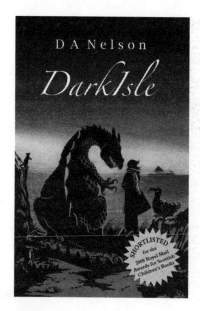

DarkIsle

ISBN 978-1-905537-04-4 (paperback, RRP £6.99)

For 10-year-old Morag, there's nothing magical about the cellar of her cruel foster parents' home. But that's where she meets Aldiss, a talking rat, and his resourceful companion, Bertie the dodo. She jumps at the chance to run away and join them on their race against time to save their homeland from the evil warlock Devlish, who is intent on destroying it. But first, Bertie and Aldiss will need to stop bickering long enough to free the only guide who knows where to find Devlish: Shona, a dragon who's been turned to stone.

Together, these four friends begin their journey to a mysterious dark island beyond the horizon, where danger and glory await—along with clues to the disappearance of Morag's parents, whose destiny seems somehow linked to her own...

'A terrific story that had me hooked from beginning to end. I *loved* it!'
D.A. Nelson, author of the award-winning *DarkIsle*

HAZEL ALLAN

Bree McCready and the Half-Heart Locket
ISBN 978-1-905537-11-2 (paperback, RRP £6.99)

Twelve-year-old Bree McCready has a mission: she has just one night to save the world!

It starts when a clue inscribed on a Half-Heart Locket leads Bree and her best friends Sandy and Honey to an ancient magical book. With it they can freeze time, fly and shrink to the size of ants.

But they soon discover the book has a long history of destruction and death. And it's being sought by the monstrous Thalofedril, who will stop at nothing to get it.

Using its incredible powers, he could turn the world into a wasteland.

Bree, Sandy and Honey go on the run—hurtling off city rooftops, down neck-breaking ravines, and through night-black underground tunnels—to keep the book out of his lethal hands. Little do they know that the greatest danger of all lies ahead, in the heart of his deadly lair...

Can Bree find the courage to face this terrifying evil, and to confront the secrets of her tragic past?

The Cat Kin
ISBN 978-1-905537-16-7 (paperback, RRP £6.99)

Everyone who came to the strange gym class was looking for something else. What they found was the mysterious Mrs Powell and Pashki, a lost art from an age when cats were worshipped as gods.

Ben and Tiffany wonder: who is their eccentric old teacher? What does she really want with them? And why are they suddenly able to see in the dark?

Meanwhile, in London's gloomy streets, human vermin are stirring. Ben and Tiffany may soon be glad of their new gifts. But against men whose cunning is matched only by their unspeakable cruelty, will even nine lives be enough?

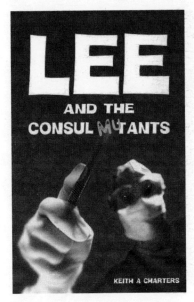

Lee and the Consul Mutants
ISBN 978-1-905537-01-3 (paperback, RRP £6.99)

It's not every day that a part of your body explodes, but Lee's appendix does exactly that, landing him in hospital.

Soon after his operation, Lee is shocked to discover that evil Consul Mutants are trying to take over the world. Worse still, the hospital he is stuck in contains the portal they are using to invade Earth.

Other kids might quake in their boots at this news, but not Lee. He's determined to save the world and comes up with a cunning plan to stop the aliens.

This is the story of a young boy battling against intergalactic odds for the sake of humankind. Lee's only weapon is his intelligence...which is a pity.

MURSU

Show this map to no one